IF YOU SEE YOUR
FATHER, SHOOT HIM

IF YOU SEE YOUR FATHER, SHOOT HIM

Carlo Morrissey

ISBN-13: 978-1721845903
ISBN-10: 1721845909

In memory of my wife Giovanna, her love was a constant that filled my days with joy.

Special thanks to my friend Hope and Cousin Lou for all your encouragement and support.

CHAPTER 1

TRICK OR TREAT

"Idiots," Mother wheezed from the living room, sitting in her black vinyl recliner, oxygen tank and walker close at hand. I imagined her slate-gray eyes casting gloom and doom. The only thing worse than Mother's eyes was her tongue. The television, her only light, played her favorite game show. Mother regained her breath and let out a raspy rant: "They let normal-looking idiots on this show. Rodney, shut off the lights and get in here before you have an army of mangy brats at the door begging for candy."

I have argued with myself thousands of times that you can be a good person and murder your mother.

"You deaf? I said shut off the..." Her voice turned into a tickle of coughs.

"In a while," I said from the kitchen, trying to get into an article on the conditions of Robert E. Lee's Army of Northern Virginia toward the end of the Civil War.

"You'll attract all those little beggars."

"I'm reading," I said, looking past the journal to a tray of bite-size candy bars I had bought for the trick-or-treaters.

"I don't care if you're writing to the president—shut off the lights!"

I know this is an awful way to live, yet I can't leave her. She is killing me, but she needs me. After her first heart attack twelve years ago and her refusal to quit smoking, I had thought that she would soon be arguing with angels about how conditions in Paradise suck. Five years ago, she stopped smoking, owing to my voiced fears over her oxygen tank, it was only a question of *when* she'd blow us up. Seven times in the last five years, doctors had announced that her passing was a matter of days. Once, it had seemed so certain that I had contacted the funeral home. But Mother has always managed to bounce back. For the last few years, I've reconciled myself to the belief Heaven is all backed up with the permanently miserable, and unless I take matters into my own hands, Mother will keep on trucking.

"Reading, writing, who gives a royal shit, those little beggars see the light, and this place will be buzzing with them."

The doorbell sounded a tinny buzz. Young, happy voices called, "Trick or treat."

"I told you those piss ants would be coming," Mother said. Then, in a hushed voice, she ordered, "Pretend you're not here. Just sit still. They'll get tired. The last thing anyone needs is to listen to strangers going on about how cute their little monsters are."

With tray in hand, I opened the door to find Janine from upstairs with her three children.

"Trick or treat," the children sang.

"Who is this guy?" I asked a small child dressed like a pirate as I deposited candies into a plastic pumpkin.

"I'm Jack from *Pirates of the Caribbean.* But it's really Davy."

Janine and I laughed. "And this little princess?" I asked.

"I'm Snow White, Mr. Armstrong."

I dropped more candy into Snow White's bucket and then bent down, smiling, at three-year-old Brittany, a.k.a. Tinker Bell.

"Getting many kids?" Janine asked.

"You guys are the first."

"I thought with it so warm, we'd get a ton." Janine smiled and whispered, "How's your mother doing?"

"Okay, you know." I shrugged. "Some days are better than others."

Janine nodded and guided her troop from the doorway, heading for the two-family's back entrance. Before they were gone, two boys about eight and ten, the bigger one wearing a football helmet and a Tom Brady Patriots jersey, the smaller guy in a Darth Vader costume, entered the hallway and shouted, "Trick or treat."

"Great costumes," I said as the boys approached with pillowcases half-filled with goodies. I examined the boys, trying to determine if I knew them. I gave them their treats and could hear Mother gasping as she traveled with her walker.

"You going to heat the whole neighborhood?" Mother said.

The boys thanked me and quickly departed.

"It's warm."

"It won't be if you keep that door open."

A moth attracted to our porch light flew near me. I waved a hand, trying to scare it away. The moth sailed over my head and into the kitchen.

"Don't wave hello—smack the bastard," Mother snapped and went inside. I turned and followed close behind, afraid she might fall. She stopped and looked down at the article I was reading. She looked back at me as if she found the article offensive. I placed the candies on the table and stiffened, readying for her best shot.

"Your grandmother once calculated if your grandfather saved the money he spent on Civil War books and other nonsense and worked another job instead of wasting his time reading that crap, he could have retired years earlier and driven a new car instead of putting around in those wrecks we hoped would get us from place to place."

"Grandma was something."

"She had a hard life," Mother said and gave a look that told me she didn't want to talk about it.

"I still remember Grandpa talking to me about all the battles and great men. He was a living encyclopedia. Gave me history lessons. Made me feel like I was right there at those battle sites. He was great. The trip you-all took to Gettysburg, when you were a kid, sounded like he had the time of his life."

"Summer." She made it sound like *phooey*. "The heat could strip the paint off your car, and horseflies, the size of quarters, thought I was lunch."

"I wish he was here. I remember us talking like it was yesterday."

"Yesterday. If he wasn't such a waster, we all would be having better tomorrows."

"I loved talking to him."

"Two dreamers."

"Everyone has dreams."

"I keep my dreams where they belong, to myself, and they stop when I open my eyes in the morning. Your dreams cost money," she said, looking down at my magazine.

"These books aren't expensive."

"Whatever they cost is too much. I'll tell you again, watch the History Channel. It's cheaper, and it'll save you time." Mother shook her head and dragged herself into the living room. "Shut off the lights before we get invaded again." The doorbell buzzed. "Too late; word is out: the Armstrong chump is giving out free candies to all the neighborhood beggars. Come one, come all to the new Hershey Palace."

Mother settled back into her easy chair for a night of TV police shows and left me alone with General Lee's battered army and the trick-or-treaters. It was a busy night by Armstrong standards as nine more groups of youngsters came calling. A little after eight thirty, three giggling girls came knocking, the last kids of the night. My Milky Ways were met with a chorus of thank-yous. The girls seemed to float down the hall and headed upstairs.

I stood for a moment and breathed in the unseasonably warm evening air. I heard Janine, back from her night of memory making, greet the trick-or-treaters. As I turned to go inside, I heard the kids thank her.

I took two steps inside, closed the door behind me, and found myself humming with the theme music from *Law & Order* that was coming from the TV. Soon, Mother would be snoring in front of the television. I looked up, made an audible gasp, and was wet-your-pants scared. Standing behind the chair I had been sitting in was a tall, overweight figure in a Batman costume, complete with gray tights, slightly torn black cape, and mask.

"You stub your toe?" Mother hollered from the living room.

Batman smiled, put a finger to his lips, and said, "It's all right."

"Who are you? What do you want?"

"Rodney, come here if you want to talk. I can't hear the television with your jabbering," Mother said, and raised the TV's volume.

The intruder said, "I think I'm here to help you."

"I don't need any help, and how did you get in here?"

"For crying out loud, Rodney, if you got something to say, get your skinny ass in here. You're ruining my show."

"Calm down," the stranger said.

"I'm calling the police."

"Only you can see and hear me."

I noticed a bright whitish glow around him. "We'll see," I said, and reached for the cell phone next to my article.

To my surprise, he did not try to stop me, only saying, "They'll think you're crazy, and it'll only make your life harder."

"Who are you?"

"Maybe you should sit down."

"Do you want money?"

"Relax, kid, I'm here to help you."

"Who are you?"

"I'm your father, Maxwell Dowling. Everyone calls me Max."

My legs shook, and I gripped a chair for support.

"I'd shake your hand, but it doesn't work that way. They tell me I'm an image. No substance."

"After all this time you come here?" I yelled. "Is this some kind of joke from the guys at work? If Van is behind this, I'll kill him. He thinks he can walk all over me, well, there's a limit. Go tell Van to go to hell, and I'll deal with him tomorrow."

"You entertaining those little beggars? I don't believe it," Mother cackled from the living room.

"I don't know any Van. I don't know where exactly I am. Only thing I know is, I'm your father, and a few minutes ago, I was in New York with the girl of my dreams—then bang, I'm here."

"Why now?"

"I didn't plan this. The dying happened on my way to a costume party," he said, and extended his arms east to west, showing a shiny purple underside to his cape. "This is all new for me too."

I reached out toward him. I should have felt material covering flesh and bone, but it was as if there was nothing before me. He shrugged. I wrapped my hands around what should have been shoulders. I saw him, but like a phantom, I could not lay hold of him. He was as he said, without substance.

"Crazy," he said.

I wanted to disappear, like the Wicked Witch in *The Wizard of Oz*, dissolve into the floor. No more Rodney—gone for good. I crumbled onto my knees and thrust my face into my hands and began rocking. I wailed, softly, not wanting to alarm Mother, "This is nuts. I never thought I'd go crazy. It's the guilt. I deserve it, I know. Dear God, please, I'm sorry. I would never actually kill her."

I heard Mother's walker and oxygen tank. I froze with fear. There she was, right before me.

"It seemed crazy to me, too, kid, but I died, and now I'm here. And I got a funny feeling I'm here for you."

"Rodney, what the hell are you doing sniffling on the floor? Are you throwing up? What the heck are you bellyaching about?"

"Mother, oh no," I moaned. Mother's heavy breathing was atop of me.

"What the hell are you bellyaching about? A grown man. You're a disgrace, carrying on like a loony bird." She nudged me with her walker.

I raised my head like a turtle venturing a look outside its shell. There she was, hovering over me. My eyes met hers, and she said, "You been hitting the coffee brandy again. I told you, at fourteen dollars a quart, I'm not sharing that with no one." Her mouth puckered and then, mockingly, said, "Poor little Rodney has nobody to play with, so he sits alone getting bombed reading boring stories about a war nobody gives a rat's ass about."

The stranger folded his arms across his chest and smiled.

"You don't see him?"

"See who?" Mother said, impatiently.

"She'll think you're crazy," he said to me.

I gulped in air like a boxer between rounds.

"Get off your knees, you damn fool. See who?"

I slowly stood, keeping my eyes on the stranger, who said to me, "Be cool, Rodney. She'll think you're nuts."

"Nobody. Who was my father?"

"Sitting Bull," she laughed, and began coughing up phlegm. She bent over her walker, tears of mirth running out of her eyes. "No, he was Standing Bull. Any way you cut it, your father was full of bull."

"Really, Mom, my father was Maxwell Dowling, right?"

The character in the Batman suit pointed to his chest and, flashing a broad grin, said, "Maxwell Dowling, at your service, son."

"He was my biggest mistake. You look like the no-good son of a bitch. He had the same you-can-trust-me eyes, caveman's forehead, sneaky nose, and wavy brown hair. You got all his genes except the nomadic ones. He was my worst nightmare."

The stranger said, shaking his head, "I can explain everything."

"Maxwell Dowling, right?"

"Why all this, and what the hell were you doing on the floor?"

"You can't tell her," he said to me.

"You were in a panic," Mother said, in a way that made me feel pathetic.

"Tell me about him!"

"What were you doing on the floor, carrying on like a lunatic?"

"I thought I saw my father."

"Where?" She straightened and took a step back.

"Don't tell her, she'll think you're crazy," Max said.

"Here."

"Here? In this house?"

"Here, trick-or-treating with, I guess, his grandkids," I said.

"Nice recovery, kid," Max told me.

"Why would you think it was your father? You've never seen the bum."

"I don't know. You said I look a lot like him."

"This guy was in his late fifties, and he looked like you? What, with a bald melon and a goofy grin, what? Tell me, please."

"No, he had a look. It was like I was seeing myself thirty years from now."

"So did you introduce yourself?"

Max began waving his arms urgently telling me to stop.

"No, but I came this close," I said; my thumb and index finger were less than a quarter inch apart.

"The kids, were they neighborhood kids?"

"Kids?"

"Hello, Rodney, you said he was with his grandkids."

"I never saw them before."

"If it was the asshole that fathered you, you're better off never seeing him again."

"Tell the bride of Frankenstein I was the best thing she ever had. I still can see the smile on her face when I left her," Max's voice hollered in my head. I cringed and put my hands over my ears.

Max scrambled behind a chair, crouching down as if trying to hide behind the seat. His jaw clenched.

He gripped the back of the chair as if in a life-and-death struggle. His shoulders hunched, and his eyes seemed locked onto a lower kitchen cabinet; then they darted up to the counter near the sink. I jumped backward as if expecting something to come crashing through the window over the sink.

"What the hell's the matter with you?" Mother yelled and began coughing again.

Max crawled under the table and peered out as if expecting trouble. He then slipped between me and Mother.

"Nothing," I said, turning from my mother and staring at Max.

"Sorry," Max said, sounding like his old self. "I got a message. Whenever I say or do something harmful, I will shrink to the size of a mouse, and a large, fat black-and-white cat will show up, looking at me like I'm a tasty, little snack."

"Wow, that's awful," I said.

"Who are you talking to?" Mother snapped.

"It's terrifying," Max said, and motioned with his head toward Mother.

"Who are you talking to?" she demanded.

"To you."

She leaned toward me and gave a good long sniff. "Rodney, I know you've been drinking. It better not be my brandy."

"No, I'm fine."

"I asked you about this mystery trick-or-treater, and you act crazy, even by your standards. And then you had your back to me and said, 'Wow, that's awful.' So who were you talking to?"

"No one."

"Good boy, deny everything," Max whispered.

"So why the jumping around, telling the wall it's terrible? You seeing things?"

"I thought I heard someone outside."

"You said, 'Wow, that's awful.' You didn't say, 'Who's there?' And before, you asked if I could see him. See who?"

"Well, maybe I'm under a lot of stress." I ran my hand through my hair and made a clucking noise with my tongue.

"Good move," Max said.

"Oh, give me a break. You work in an air-conditioned store selling overpriced suits to snobby assholes. You haven't a clue what stress is. Try living knowing you should have been dead ten years ago. That's the trouble with your whole generation, a little pressure and you collapse like a beach chair at sunset."

"Well, whatever it is, Mom, I need to know about my father."

"Your father?"

"Yes."

"He was a rat bastard. His only talent was destroying lives."

"Was it all bad?"

She looked me up and down and screamed, "Maxwell Dowling, my curse."

Max shook his head.

"Can't be." I shook my head and muttered, over and over, slinking into a chair across from my mother, who looked at me with more than her normal level of disgust.

"You seeing that shrink?"

"You know I am."

"See if you can get your money back because you're getting worse." She started to drag herself back to the living room. Then she stopped and turned toward me and said, "Don't go bonkers on me, Rodney. I'm counting on you to give me a proper send-off, and the way I feel, it could be any day. Knowing you'll be around so the undertaker and the state don't screw with me after I'm stuffed in a box is the only reassuring thought I got. So at least wait until I'm six feet under before you loosen any more of your screws." Mother lifted her walker an inch off the floor and started again for the living room. "Tell me you're okay, Rodney."

"I'm okay," I said, relieved she was leaving us.

"I still don't know why you were on the floor."

"I didn't want to say, but I was praying."

"Beautiful, kid, simply beautiful," Max told me.

"For what, a personality?"

"It's personal."

"Call Dr. What's-His-Face."

"Hitchfield."

"Call him in the morning, and see if he can give you something that works."

I nodded.

"What were you seeing?"

"Nothing; I'm under a lot of stress. It probably was just the way the light was hitting on the window that made him seem like an older me."

"Baloney, but here's something that's real, in my closet, on the shelf under an oversize Christmas sweater with dancing Santas, I keep your grandfather's pistol. Check it out. Make sure it works, and if that lousy bastard you saw is Maxwell Dowling, and if he has the nerve to bring his shameless ass here, you call me because there is nothing that would please me more before I kick off than to put a bullet between his eyes."

CHAPTER 2

ONE IN A MILLION

Max and I watched Mother make her way to the recliner. Soon she would be snoozing in front of the television. We agreed not to talk—or rather I wouldn't speak, and he wouldn't send me messages until Mother sent us a steady stream of snores. I stared at the magazine article. Robert E. Lee's problems were no competition for my Batman. The longer we sat in silence, the worse I felt about whatever it was sitting across from me. Max amused himself with his cape, motioning as if he were a matador eluding invisible bulls.

After a while I got up and looked in on Mother. Her head was resting on her left shoulder. The creases in her oxygen-starved skin were a dark gray. Gently, her thin blue lips flapped. Her nose jiggled a bit as a chorus of snores gained momentum in her throat. I walked over to the sofa and lifted a pink-and-white afghan. As if protecting fine china, I draped the afghan around her shoulders and loosely tucked it under her hips. Mother half opened her eyes and gave me the start of a smile. From years of practice, I knew if I shut off the television, she would scream, "I'm watching that."

"She out," Max asked.

I nodded and whispered, "Let's give it a few minutes."

"Everyone calls me Max."

I put a finger to my mouth, indicating it was too soon for conversation. The last thing I wanted was to get friendly with the ghost of the jerk who had fathered me.

"Don't worry she can't hear me. I could do a jig on her head, and she wouldn't be any the wiser. I'm gone, nothing, to everyone but you. Slowly, what I'm about, what this is about, is coming to me. And, Rodney, my man, you are my connection with this life." Max lifted his cape and made a dramatic bow.

Lucky me, I thought, and whispered, "I don't get it."

"I'm not one hundred percent sure, myself," Max said, and leaned back in his chair. "I was told, by this very sexy-sounding voice, 'You have a son. His name is Rodney Armstrong. Go.' If I wasn't already dead, I would have had a heart attack! But there I was, lying on the carpet at Penny Colvin's feet, dead. And this voice is commanding me to go, and ta-da, here I am. Penny was hot, oh so hot, in her Catwoman costume. That's what killed me."

"An erotic voice sent you?"

"Right, I mean that's who she sounded like. Real sexy but firm, the kind of voice you can't ignore. See, I'm the kind of man that if a guy tells me something, unless I'm in trouble or trying to scam him out of something, I don't really listen. Now, I hear a lady's voice, and bang, I'm all eyes and ears. It's like I'm hardwired to listen to them. It's always been like that for me. I figure I'm always thinking about my next, and this is hard to say to my son, especially knowing your opinion of me must be lower than dirt after a lifetime with Audrey, the queen of battle-axes." He paused and looked at me as if wanting to hear an opposing view.

Max was right on the money. I wanted to yell at him and heap insults, but with Mother sawing logs in the next room, I instead shot him looks that I hoped betrayed my disgust and asked, "Your next what?"

"Oh, you know."

I stared blankly at him.

"You know, jelly roll, bury the salami, jump on her bones. I was a man who got up every day looking for a good time and wanting that good time to be with a lady friend who didn't put limits on me, someone who was glad to see me go when the sun came up. A good time on the cheap. I was, eh…"

"A lowlife."

Max wiggled uncomfortably in his chair and said, "I see it more like I wasn't ready to settle down."

"How old are you?"

"Fifty-seven. That seems old to you, but I felt more like twenty-seven than fifty-seven. My way of looking at it was I could get serious about life tomorrow."

"And now you're dead."

Max nodded.

"So how is that?"

"Being dead?"

I nodded.

"Except for the hungry cat scaring the crap out of me, it isn't bad." He hesitated, and his tone became far more serious. "I don't know what to expect, but the longer I'm in this world of being nothing to anyone except to you, I feel better." He paused, and I think he was trying to sound sympathetic, but I was concentrating on his spare tire and flabby legs, which looked ridiculous in the clingy Batman body suit. "I'm sorry for having abandoned you and your mother. I wasn't ready to be a father. I'm still not ready. Back then, I got scared when Audrey hit me with the news. I was only looking for a good time, never a family, or even romance. Something funny, kid?"

"The suit seems tight."

"That's what killed me. I had the hots bad for Penny. She's forty-five, believed I was forty-eight, working as a Defense Department analyst. I learned about ten years ago that women are impressed with men involved in defending their country, community, anything where you put your life on the line for others. Being a lifesaver makes them feel safe or something." He gave a little chuckle that made me want to throw him out. "Since I never was in the military, and being out of shape, I'd look stupid in a uniform, I settled for the next best thing, Defense Department. See, if the lady starts asking too many questions, all's you got to do is tell her, 'Can't get into that, top secret. With Penny we were at a point that all I had to say was TS."

"TS?"

"Top secret. It was great, all kinds of respect I milked off of that job. I could use it to avoid things, you know, if I needed a break from Penny or wanted to try my luck with some strange pussy, just tell her, 'It's work, don't know how long I'll be gone.'"

"A job you never had?"

"Right, but she was none the wiser." Max smiled and continued, "There were things we did that are still illegal in twelve states. One night she got on top of me, and she had these magnificent long legs, and she was into dance aerobics. Wow, could she move. She starts to…" Suddenly Max leaped out of his seat and crouched next to me. I could see his arms wrapped around my legs but felt nothing. Then, just as quickly, he stood up and apologized profusely.

"The cat?" I asked.

"Was up on the table ready to swallow me whole. If I wasn't dead, I'd have wet myself."

"Maybe we should talk about something else," I said, and he nodded. "You were never curious about what happened to my mother?"

"No, I was hoping she found someone else. Your mother was a real looker. Va-va-voom. One thing no one ever could say is Max Dowling ever dated a dog."

I gave him a disappointed look.

"Okay your mother. Hey, she was a kid. Your mother had one of those lean bodies with enough meat on her that you knew you had a girl and not some skinny boy." He then sat back into his seat and folded his arms. "The first time I met her, she was having trouble starting her car. A '65 Ford Fairlane. I had jumper cables, and she was someone worth helping. She had a skirt that hugged her fanny, and it was having fun doing it. And the little smile she gave me when I offered to help. Man, I was ready to roll with her all day and night. It's hard to believe she's the same woman." He motioned with his head toward the living room.

"Maybe your coming here leads to me killing you again."

"Shit, kid, I don't know what's going to happen, but I think you should know the circumstances that brought you into this world. So, where was I? Right, I said to myself, 'I'm going to have some fun tonight—yes, Max, this girl's for you.'" He shook his shoulders excitedly.

Before I could protest, Max jumped out of his chair again and squeezed himself behind a potted yucca plant that stood to one side near the entrance to the living room. He lowered his head so that only the top of his cap and bat ears showed behind the giant yucca.

"What the hell? Oh no," I said, realizing he was dealing with the cat.

"Sorry, sorry, sorry," Max apologized, and slowly stood up. He sheepishly stepped around the plant and returned to his chair. "That cat was inches from me. I could smell its breath." He shuddered.

"That wasn't helpful."

"I know, but that night with your mother was memorable. And that's a compliment to your mother."

"Listen, asshole. You wrecked her life, never thought about me all this time, and now you show up here and want to brag about banging my mother. Where's that cat?"

"That's it!" he shouted in my head.

"That's it. That's what?"

"You love your mother. She talks to you like you're a four-year-old who messed his pants, yet you still love her."

"You don't know what you're talking about."

"I know I'm here for a reason. And I think that reason is to help you. Because thirty-five years ago I harpooned your mom. I think it's deeper than that, Rodney. I'm not a deep guy—even after dying I don't think I'm going to gain a whole lot of insights, but this is it. It's got to be. And no more talk about sex; you notice whenever you get me started on sex, the next thing I know I'm looking up at a hungry Garfield."

"It's you who brings it up."

"I do?"

I nodded and said, "So I love my mother."

"Right, because I hear the way she talks to you. No way would you take that unless you loved her."

"What do you know?" I could feel my anger rising, and I waved an arm at him as if trying to knock his words back.

"I know I'm here, and the only reason I could be here is to help the son I abandoned. And what I see is somebody who needs a lot of help. What I see is an uptight guy living with his dying mother. A mother who, and maybe I came on an off night, has the disposition of a cornered wolf."

"Uptight!"

"Sure, look at you. It's Halloween, and instead of rocking with some sweet babe at a party, you're passing out candy, reading about a war that everyone knows how it ends. And those glasses you going for the nerdy look?"

I raised my eyebrows and defensively removed my dark-framed spectacles, shook my head, and snarled.

"No offense, but the last guy who got any mileage out of that look was Buddy Holly, and he's been dead more than fifty years."

I sat back, put the glasses on my nose, and felt the blood trying to pound through my skull.

"And that shirt, you look like you're ready to do my taxes. Unless you're going to put on a tie, unbutton the frigging top button. And looking you over, your hands, they look like they never lifted anything heavier than a pencil. Again, unless you're a professor or scientist, the girls see you and they either feel sorry for you or forget you before you said hello."

Max looked up at the ceiling and shouted, "Are you sure this is the right kid?" Then he flinched and nodded repeatedly. "Sorry, the voice just scolded me. They don't make mistakes, and I'm beginning to wear out their patience. I guess if we don't make progress soon, Garfield will be munching on big Max." He pointed to himself with a thumb and shrugged. "So tell me, Rodney, you getting any?"

"I don't think that's any of your business."

"Just what I thought."

"How's that important?"

"If you got to ask, then this is a bigger problem than I imagined."

I narrowed my eyes and tried to look pissed.

"Now don't start crying on me. But when was the last time you had a date?"

"I don't see how that matters." I felt my face redden. I remembered Kimberly Eagleton and our senior prom. We were both in the history, chess, yearbook, and math clubs. It had taken me three years to get up the courage to ask her out, two months before the prom. I still remember when she said yes. It had been before our Honors Advanced Statistics class. She had been wearing a dark-green dress covered in black butterflies. She had smiled and straightened her eyeglasses. After graduation, she had left for a summer institute at Johns

Hopkins University, where she had had a scholarship for the fall. I had stayed local. We were going to stay in touch. Kimberly had come home for Thanksgiving, and I had invited her over for pie and coffee after her family had finished its holiday feast. Mother had polished off more coffee brandy than turkey. She had explained to Kimberly the facts of life, namely that if she were smart she would look for a man with money, of which her Rodney had none. Mother had then gone into my potential to make money. She had summed me up as being doomed to a life of clipping newspaper coupons.

Mother had been relentless in running me down, and I had done nothing to defend myself. When she had finally announced that it was getting late, 9:30, and Kimberly had to leave, I had seen my first and last opportunity for love run out as if the place had been infested with giant cockroaches.

"Now I'm going to give you a lesson in the basics. You are a man, right?"

I nodded.

"And despite the life you've been living, you still have my genes in you. What I'm saying is, for a man, any man, to be happy, you have to have a woman around who enjoys your manliness. And being my son, that goes at least double."

"Why do you think I'm not happy?"

"You tell me. Are you happy?"

"That's not a simple question."

Max groaned.

"No, really, when I'm at work and a customer appreciates the service I give him, I feel good, really good, like I know I've made a difference. There's a look they give me."

"What the hell is it that you do?"

"I sell men's clothes at Haynesworth and Waite's."

"Get real, Rodney. Do you think when your customers go out and someone says, 'Nice suit,' do you think they say, 'My man Rodney suggested it?' Do you think if you're not there the guy is going to skip buying what he needs? Boy, you've got to be kidding me. Don't give yourself so much credit, none of us is that important."

"What I do know is I have my customers, and they always ask for me. Do you know, Jags Carmello won't let anyone else wait on him?"

"Jags who?"

"Carmello. He just beat murder and racketeering charges. Newspapers called him a major player in New England's organized crime."

"I don't care if President Obama flies in special to get fitted by you."

I made the start of a pout.

"Fine, I'll give you that you're the man when it comes to picking out ties. But does that sound like a ringing endorsement of a happy life? 'I feel good when I sell a stranger a suit.'"

"They're not strangers." I tried to sound like he didn't have a clue, but I felt defensive and probably sounded that way.

"So these customers, you go to ball games with them or catch a brew after work with them? They have you over for dinner, right?" There was a pause. I wanted to tell him to screw.

"Hey, kid, don't start weeping on me. I know you only see these customers at work. So tell me what makes you happy."

I stood, unbuttoned my shirt, and paced back and forth from the sink to the table, beginning to feel as miserable as Mother sounded. I dropped into my chair and in a defeated voice, said, "When I think about times with my grandfather, I feel so lucky to have had him in my life. He was always glad to see me."

"That's nice. How long has he been dead?"

"Fifteen years."

"So you got people glad they bought a shirt from you and memories of Grandpa from when you were a kid. Yeah, sounds like you should write a book on the secrets to a happy life."

"That's not all."

"Don't tell me you love to watch the sunset."

"No, but I do like to dream about things." I told myself not to let this ghost get to me. I knew once Mother was gone, I would start living. But I felt a chill of fear at the thought of sharing with Max the joy I felt on planning for life after Mother. "The best thing is thinking about my dream vacation."

"Listen to you. Are you seventy-five or thirty-five?"

I recoiled.

"Talk to me. This dream vacation…when are you leaving, and who are you going with?"

"I plan on going on a four or five-week trip to all of the major battle sites of the Civil War. I'll start at Gettysburg and work my way south."

"That's it?"

"I love that time in our history. I know all about the battles, from Bull Run to Appomattox. I've considered writing a book on what Lee did wrong. Some of the most critical battles have been cheated out of their rightful place in history. The amazing stories of Cold Harbor and Fredericksburg need to be told in a way that ends their place as second bananas to Gettysburg and Vicksburg."

"Wonderful. Listen, the last thing you need is to be sitting all alone writing a book. What you need is a girl-friend. And you better get started before you become too weird and have to settle for a girl who needs a green card and lots of dental work."

"You're crazy."

"I'm crazy? Then let me ask you, this dream vacation of southern cemeteries, are you going with a friend?"

"No," I snapped.

"When are you leaving?"

"I don't know. It would have to be after Mother passes. She could never handle the stress, and she's not good with change. Her caretaker, Elizabeth, stays with her during the day, but it would be too much for her to stay over. And I'm not sure if I would ever get all that time off at once. I only get two weeks off, and the only exceptions are for marriages or something like that."

"So you get excited about planning a vacation you'll never take?"

"I wouldn't say never," I said, feeling foolish.

"Sounds like it to me." Max shook his head and asked, "Tell me about Elizabeth."

"She's Mother's personal care attendant."

"What's she like?"

"She can move mountains."

"Move mountains?"

"She won Mother over in a matter of days."

"That was a big deal?"

"Mother wanted her out the first day, refused to let Elizabeth help her with anything. By the third day, Mother said, 'She's not half bad.' Before the week was out, Mother was looking forward to Elizabeth being with her. She's about your age, from Jamaica, a big woman, so happy it's contagious." I thought about how lucky we were to have her.

"Okay, so let's get back to you. Rodney, you're not living. You're only going through the motions."

"You don't understand."

"Explain."

"I can't do anything until Mother dies. The last time I brought a girl here, it was a disaster. I won't do that again. I could have killed Mother."

"What did you do?"

I felt totally inadequate as I said, "Nothing."

"Number one thing—it just came to me like a neon sign flashing in my brain. You've got to start telling your mother how you feel about things. You got to stop letting her walk all over you. You're the man of the house."

"I—I—I can't."

"Why? You afraid?"

"No, there's just no talking to my mother. She's relentless. Even now she'll chew me up and spit me out."

"You are afraid of her."

"No, I'm afraid if I argued with her, I could kill her. That's what I'm afraid of, the very thing that makes me happy. No more Mother, but the thought of me causing her death…" I shuddered. "I couldn't live with myself. I'm okay planning something that will never happen, like getting Jags to bump her off. I guess I know it won't happen, but daydreaming about it gives me a sense of solving the problem. I need that until she dies."

"You love her."

"Of course I do; it's just I know she's suffering. We're both suffering. It would be different if there was some chance of her getting better. But this just goes on and on, and each month she becomes a little weaker and a little nastier."

Suddenly, a crumbled piece of paper hit my nose, and I was seized with terror. Next to Max, hunched over her walker, stood Mother.

"What the hell are you blabbering about?"

Max smiled and gave a thumbs-up sign.

I swallowed hard. "You okay?"

"You're talking to yourself?"

"No." It was an automatic response, like when a five-year-old is caught licking frosting from an uncut cake.

"Well, how the hell did I hear, 'Each month she becomes a little weaker, a little nastier'? What is it, you already counting the life insurance money? Already have me planted?"

"No, what I said was, 'Each month they become a little weaker; it was nasty.'"

"What the hell are you talking about?"

"The Army of Northern Virginia."

"Nice move, kid," Max said.

"I may have a ticker that couldn't power a squirrel and lungs that stopped working right sometime during the Clinton administration, but my hearing is still good, you inconsiderate little bastard, so if you're praying for me to kick the bucket, keep it to yourself because I'm not ready to go anywhere."

"It's the book I told you I want to write about the Civil War. I was thinking out loud. I get so excited about it. That article has me juiced up."

"Stick to that story," Max said, giving me an okay sign.

"I don't believe it. And you're starting to worry me. First, you're on your knees ready to bawl your eyes out, then you're talking to the walls, and now you're, what, praying about how bad you got it? You asking God to take me? Boo-hoo-hoo." She raised her hands to her eyes and pretended to be crying.

"No, believe me, I was thinking about a book project."

"Give that shrink a call in the morning."

"I'm okay, really."

"Maybe I should call him...what's-his-face...Hitch-field. If you're losing it, at least be man enough to keep it to yourself like the rest of us." Mother looked me up and down, her eyes full of disgust as she said, "You thinking about getting a disability as a nutcase?"

"No!"

"Then you better get to bed if you're going to work in the morning."

I nodded and stood. Mother crept toward her bedroom. I went around the apartment checking windows and doors, with Max following a step behind. He told me not to speak until I was certain Mother was sleeping.

"Just listen, Rodney," he said as I unfolded the bedcovers. "I know it's hard for you to realize you're afraid, but I know now that's how I'm supposed to help you."

I walked past Max, gave him a skeptical look, and closed the bedroom door. "By making my mother think I'm nuts?" I whispered.

"Shush—you don't want her hearing you."

"Don't shush me."

"You're the guy who doesn't want her thinking you're ready for the cracker factory."

"So where are you going now?"

"No place. I'm with you, buddy, until they decide it's over. I hope my next stop is heaven, but I think I'll have to straighten out some other screw-ups I've made. I'm getting this image of my brother, who I went into business with…a gas station. He did all the work. I stole about thirty grand from him. He never suspected anything. Stood by me. We sold the place after two years, and I made another twenty grand from the liquidation. It ruined him, cost him his marriage. Your mother is right I'm a rat bastard, was a rat bastard. But you know, Rodney, I'm feeling better the longer I'm here."

"Well, whippy-doo, but you're not staying here?"

"I have no choice, kid. I didn't come here. I was deposited, presto!"

"I can't sleep with you here."

"Then we can talk as long as you don't start yelling and wake up Mrs. Frankenstein."

I shook my head and put on my pajamas, a blue-diamond pattern.

"I knew you were a PJ guy. I'm a jump-into-bed-in-my-boxers guy." Max started to get into the bed.

"Don't you dare!"

He backed off and stood next to me wearing a silly grin.

"Tell me how you died," I whispered.

"I was a madman, Rodney. I lived all my life on the edge, pushing the odds. There's nothing I did that I'm proud of." Max shook his head as if surprised at himself. "I can't believe I said that. I used to think I lived the way most only dreamed about."

"The day you died?" I asked, feeling sorry for him as one does for a lost cause that might have been very different if only. Except, I think, in Max's case, there would be hundreds of if-onlys.

"I was snorting cocaine not a lot, just enough to feel it. Penny came home all excited. She'd picked up our costumes, Batman and Catwoman. I wasn't in the mood to play dress-up. We were going to her friend's house for a party. To Penny's friends I was a mystery man, you know, working on top secret assignments. I was real horny—just looking at her fingernails was getting me excited. So she plants a big smooch on my cheek and drops this silly outfit on the couch next to me. I tell her, 'Let's go later.' She gives me these big sad dog eyes and runs into the bedroom with her costume. She knew I can't stand her being down." Max shrugged and continued. "'It'll be a blast,' she says. I look at the Batman outfit and yelled at her, 'I can't wear this—it's got frigging tights.'

"'Of, course it does; you're Batman,' she said from the bedroom. I can hear the ceiling fan starting in the bedroom and her getting undressed. I'm thinking, 'Go in there and toss her on the bed. The hell with the party.' I head for the bedroom. Penny is just pulling up her Catwoman tights, and she purrs, real sexy. Hell, I didn't need any encouragement. I wrap my arms around her middle from behind and slip my hands down her panties. She elbows me in the gut and says, 'If I get a run in my tights, I'll die.' If she only knew who was going to die.

"I let go, and she says, 'See how it fits.' I complain about not wanting to wear the tights, and she yells, 'You told me get something that's really masculine; you can't get more macho than Batman. Now put it on, or I'll go by myself.' So I figure the only way I'm scoring with my little lady is if I put the stupid suit on. I do. She's all dressed in like ten seconds. Her tail is curled, sticking up in the back, driving me crazy. You got to remember, Penny is a knockout and now with that suit on, mama mia. She starts helping me with the suit. Big problems for me my dick is saluting, like I OD'd on Viagra. I mean, I was aroused before Penny came home and had only one thing on my mind, and it wasn't playing the caped crime fighter. Penny gives me a smile and tells me to quiet little Max. I'm thinking I'll explode if I don't get the damn stockings off. Wow. I'm afraid any movement will launch little Max's armada. Because I'm not moving, letting Penny fix my cape, she thinks my desires have cooled. The mask goes on, and Penny, tail wagging playfully, says, 'Maybe we can leave early and give each other a treat.'

"I couldn't take it anymore. I was the wrong guy to be in that getup with someone as hot as Penny." Max shuddered.

"So what did you do?"

"What else could I do? I grabbed her by the shoulders and flipped the cape, which was tied around my neck with a velvet cord. Penny's natural reaction was to push me away. I've got my arms raised, spreading the cape like Dracula did in those old movies. The cape, and this has got to be a one-in-a-million shot, got caught on one of the ceiling fan's blades and lifted me for about a second off the ground. There I was, a flying Batman. Well, I'm two hundred and thirty pounds, and all of me, tied to a ceiling fan, is trying desperately to spread Penny across her bed. I think the fan's screws must have been loose. Because faster than you can say kaboom, the fan comes tearing out of the ceiling. The motor, a heavy sucker, makes a direct hit, right here." Max pointed to the middle of his skull. "Now the fan had moved me a few feet, so when the motor hit my squash, my face came crashing into the bedpost. It's a Colonial-style bed—solid maple. The posts have these balls the size of coconuts adorning their tops. Somehow the post smashed through my head. I was dead in a blink. I saw Penny, horrified. It looked like she was screaming, but I couldn't hear her. Then I started getting chewed out by that voice, and—bam! I found myself in your kitchen. Weird doesn't even begin to describe it."

I gave a big yawn and said, "So you got killed trying to rape your girlfriend?"

"Boy, talk about putting a negative spin on things."

"Just saying that's what it sounds like."

"I think I'll revise the story."

"Okay," I said and drifted off to sleep.

CHAPTER 3

MIDNIGHT CHICKEN

I opened my eyes to Max's nose an inch from mine. He put a finger to his lips and reminded me of my need not to spark Mother's interest. He lowered his hand and smiled down at me the way a victor gloats over the vanquished.

"Shit, you're still here."

"Shush, don't want to get Audrey in here asking who you're talking to now." He gave a contented little sigh and said, "I was hoping I'd moved on too. But the night passed like this." Max snapped his fingers. "You know what's really crazy about being dead? Even now that nothing can kill me, I'm afraid of dying. That's why the giant cat is so scary. We must spend a whole lot of time acting out of fear. At first I thought it was just you who was Mr. Uptight." He shrugged. "It's probably everyone. Just most of us fake it a lot better than you."

"Please, I think I'm doing pretty good talking to a ghost."

He nodded.

"You've been here all night?" I stretched my arms and rolled my neck.

"You know, you make a little chirping noise when you're sleeping. It's like when food is trying to escape out your mouth, and your tongue is trying to lick it back in, but its dealing with a mouthful of drink on top of the stuff you got to chew, so it's between a gulp and a chirp, not really a snore. And do you know, every once in a while you growl."

"Never noticed what I do when I'm sleeping." I stretched some more and quietly despaired over seeing Max. I had hoped somewhere in my dreams that last night would have merged into never-never land, and I would spend my morning sitting over coffee thinking, did my father, disguised as Batman, really come see me, or was it just the most vivid dream ever? But no luck—there he was, the sorriest excuse of a Batman I could ever imagine. Worse, if it could get any worse. I could see myself under this screwball ghost's mask. The resemblance was uncanny. So that's me in twenty years, another victim of gravity and a sedentary life. I'm seeing my future self in a degenerative ghost. "I need Dr. Hitchfield."

"Shush, you don't want her in here cross-examining you. Not feeling so good?"

I nodded.

Sounding a bit sad, Max said, "Maybe after breakfast you'll feel better." He then continued, more to himself, "I wish they told me what to expect. But somehow it's not that big a deal. Here I am tied to you, and it's not really that bad. If this is hell, then you're in it with me."

"Lucky me." I felt bad after saying this and in a kinder tone, said, "Believe me, it's not hell." Max screwed up his mouth. I wanted to reassure him. "It's life on earth for all of us except you." Ah shit, as soon as it came out, I knew I was making things worse. "I'm sure whatever this is, it's going to end soon." I got out of bed and listened for sounds of life in the kitchen. "You're still invisible to everyone else?"

Max nodded and said, "I guess. I've been here all night watching you sleep. It's amazing when you conked out, it was like I was frozen in place. I didn't have a care in the world. You wake up, and it's like I woke up too, right away my head starts buzzing with thoughts about you."

We whispered small talk, which seemed surprisingly normal, reinforcing my need to see Dr. Hitchfield. I got clean underwear and socks and headed for the shower but stopped short when I saw Max following me. He explained again how he automatically travels with me, that he has to be in the same room, and promised that he would stay as far away as possible in the bathroom and not check me out. After showering and shaving, I took over the kitchen, making a breakfast of scrambled eggs and pancakes. I always ate heavy before work, preferring to use my lunch for appointments or to take a walk. On workdays, I always made extra pancakes or French toast because Elizabeth loved my breakfasts.

Elizabeth had come to America fifteen years earlier with her husband, James, who worked as a maintenance man at the St. Benedict's Nursing Home. A big woman, Elizabeth had been with us for three years. She did some housecleaning, made Mother lunch on days when she felt like eating, and gave me peace of mind when I was at work. Elizabeth was a talker and a big fan of the daytime soaps. Mother complained about me throwing money away, paying to have someone eat all our food and yak all day about who's sleeping with who on her soap opera. But I knew my mother really enjoyed the company.

It hadn't always been that way. At first Mother had refused to let Elizabeth help her, but in time she had softened to the big housekeeper, who had been just as relentless in her determination to care for Mother as Mother had been determined to resist the help.

After the second day of Elizabeth's employment with us, I had sat her down to tell her that it wasn't working since Mother had refused to eat anything Elizabeth had prepared and had refused to allow the woman to touch her. "I warned you that my mother can be extremely difficult. Don't take it as something you did," I had started to tell her.

Elizabeth had shaken her head no.

"Well, she's the kind of person who feels better complaining and arguing than having a good time. I'm afraid it'll only get worse. I think we'll have to let you go."

"Mr. Armstrong, you are a very kind man. I can tell by the way you treat your mother and the way you talk to me." With a broad smile, she had continued, "Your mother needs help, and you need help with her. It is hard when we are dying slowly to let go and let others in to help. I will always respect her, but I will also always help her. My mother took care of Mr. William of the sugar plantation. He was like your mother. Mad for dying yet not happy for living. Mama showed me how to help the dying despite their fear and anger." Elizabeth had looked up toward the ceiling and said, "It will not always be like today." Then she had looked me in the eye and in the sweetest, richest voice imaginable had said, "She will not defeat my heart. Let me help the both of you." Within the week Elizabeth was helping Mother dress and bathe.

Elizabeth entered, carrying two big brown shopping bags. I momentarily panicked. What if she could see Max? Before she fully entered, she said, almost singing the words, "Mr. Armstrong, Miss Armstrong I did not see you there; here are the last of my tomatoes that I promised. The big ones have a spot of yellow; the small ones are like green walnuts, but keep them in the bag on the windowsill, and in three days, the yellow ones will be pink, and the green ones yellow. The rest is what I need to make midnight chicken like I promised. How are you today, my treasure?" Elizabeth said, gently caressing Mother's shoulders.

"Couldn't sleep," Mother said, poking at her pancakes as if expecting something to crawl out from under them.

"Why, my dear Miss Armstrong?" Elizabeth asked, unloading her bags: two big chickens, cloves, honey, a can of crushed pineapple, dried spearmint, a bottle of rosemary, a box of brown sugar, six large yams, a package of fresh mushrooms, three yellow squashes, and a quart of dark rum.

I was at the stove lifting the last of the pancakes off the skillet and hollered, "You going to feed an army?"

"Once a year I make my midnight chicken. It is so good you will want to eat it all week. You will want to share with your friends and get drunk and talk all night. That is why we call it midnight chicken, because when we make it, come midnight we are just starting to have some fun. With this dinner we always have great fun; that is why my mother so loved it. That is why I make it every year on her birthday. Thank you, Mama," Elizabeth said, and looked up at the ceiling for a moment."

"You want eggs?" I asked, sliding a dish with four golden brown pancakes in front of her.

"Only if you have enough," she said, holding her stomach. "My James can eat no more eggs. His cholesterol is going through the roof. Me, I can eat whatever, and nothing changes. I told him he does not breathe right." Elizabeth inhaled deeply, and her bosom jumped. "This is how you must breathe, I tell him, and he waves his hand at me like it's my fault he can't eat eggs or ham or ice cream." Then she asked Mother again, "What's wrong?"

"Rodney is getting ready for the loony bin. Look at him; he shouldn't have a care in the world, but he's cracking up. I caught him on his knees crying like his nose got caught in the door. Then he's talking to the walls. And before he went to bed, he's talking to God about how I'm falling apart. and I'm sure he's asking God to do him a favor and punch my ticket for the great by-and-by." Mother looked at her pancake suspiciously and said, "I've been waiting for you to test the food—not sure if my assassin son decided on taking matters into his own hands."

"You're nuts, Mom," I said, scooping up some pancake from her plate and dropping it into my mouth in dramatic fashion. I closed my eyes and slowly chewed, savoring every morsel.

"What is this all about?" Elizabeth asked, looking up at me.

"Be cool, Rodney," Max said.

"Last night, I saw an older man who looked like me. I thought maybe he was my father."

"Be careful, kid," Max said.

"It explains nothing," Mother said, taking a small bite of her food.

"I'm also excited about an idea for a book."

"A book," Elizabeth said. "How very interesting. You are a very talented man. I told my James about the books and magazines you read. I said, 'Mr. Rodney's mind is always working.'"

"Don't start ordering copies," Mother said; "he only has an idea and as much ability as those tomatoes you brought us."

"Everything begins with an idea," Elizabeth said.

"Don't encourage him," Mother yelled.

"What is the book about?" Elizabeth asked.

"The—" I started.

"It's a surprise-ending autobiography," Mother interrupted. "How Rodney Armstrong drove himself crazy. The surprise part is that he doesn't realize what a short trip it is."

"I would have smothered her years ago," Max whispered.

"That is terrible, Miss Audrey," Elizabeth said.

Max suddenly dropped to his knees and crawled under the table. I could see his head bobbing around Elizabeth's lap.

I gulped and said, "I'd like to write about some of the important Civil War battles that haven't gotten as much attention as they should."

Max unraveled himself from under the table and in a frightened whisper, said, "The cat."

I nodded absentmindedly.

"It sounds like a fine idea," Elizabeth said.

"I'm the one dying," Mother said, pointing a forkful of pancake at me; "if anyone is supposed to be going nuts, it's me." The veins in her neck started twitching.

"You are beating all the odds," I said. "I bet you'll bury your doctors."

"Laughing at the reaper takes courage," Elizabeth said. "You are a fierce fighter, battling always, never forgiving or asking to be forgiven."

"Forgiving for what?" Mother asked.

"For being human, like all of us."

"Eat your pancakes," Mother snapped, pulling on her powder-blue robe, which seemed heavy on her bony frame.

"They are delicious. And tonight I will make a very special dinner. It is the birthday of my mother, God bless her soul. Like I told you last week, my James is working late, so we will have a little feast. It is not good to eat alone on special days. This recipe was my mother's favorite. The chicken is roasted in honey, rum, and brown sugar. The yams will be so sweet your teeth will hurt, but your belly will smile."

"Sounds like a hell of a lot of work for you, me, and Rodney."

"I will take some home for James, and like I said, you will want to eat it all week."

"I thought you told me you were dirt-poor," Mother said.

"We were," Elizabeth said, smiling as she loaded her pancakes with maple syrup.

"And you could eat like that?" Mother said.

"Only on special days, birthdays, Christmas. The rest of the year, we ate beans and rice, beans and bread, beans and yams, beans…"

"Got it, you ate a lot of freaking beans," Mother interrupted.

Elizabeth nodded and turned her attention to her breakfast. After a few minutes, Mother tried to push back her chair to stand but was too weak. Elizabeth quickly got up to help. Mother turned to her and said, "I'm tired; I need to sleep, thanks to sonny boy over there."

"Well, I'm going to walk to work today, so I'll be leaving in a few minutes. You need anything, Elizabeth?

Mother looked at me and said, "When you come home tonight, you better come clean about what the hell was going on last night. The truth, mister."

I took two deep breaths and said, "Okay, okay. Truth is, I've been worried sick about you. I was praying, praying for your recovery, praying that you'll be at peace. I didn't want to scare you. Maybe you should see a priest."

"Be careful, kid," Max whispered, standing behind me.

"My priest is a man of great kindness and love, Rodney," Elizabeth said. "His voice can calm a lion."

"Where was he working before the circus?" Mother cackled.

"He runs an outreach program for men returning from prison and a food pantry in the Cushing Square area. He works so hard running our parish and then all the extra things. He's such a good man."

"Why not see him?" I said, thinking that anyone who hung around the Cushing Square neighborhood and saw convicts in his free time might be a match for Mother.

"You two, ha," Mother said, flipped her head sideways, and began walking to her bedroom. Elizabeth hovered behind her, threw me a wink, and smiled over her shoulder.

CHAPTER 4

BEATRICE, DINKY, AND SPIKE

I was greeted outside by an unseasonably warm first day of November. I looked around, soaking in the beautiful blue sky, and hoped Max was gone, but there he was on my left a half step behind me.

"How long of a walk?" Max asked.

"Takes about forty minutes."

"No car?"

"I try to walk as much as I can. You know, save energy, help the planet, curb global warming, economize, and get some exercise." I felt like I was defending my life.

"I'm getting the picture that I fathered a bookworm environmental wacko who's afraid of his mommy."

"I'm not afraid of her!" I shouted.

"Hey, cool it. You don't want people seeing a well-dressed lunatic yelling at no one."

I stopped dead in my tracks and looked all around. The nearest people were two young mothers pushing baby carriages half a block behind us.

"Think we should drive?"

"I think you should leave because I really have enough going on without having a ghost with a bad attitude tagging along."

"Bad attitude?"

"Bookworm environmental wacko? I just don't need to hear that from a guy who says he's my father."

"Was your father."

"Well, nice meeting you after thirty-five years. Sorry about the accident now have a nice eternity." Max looked at me like I had three heads. "Shove off. I don't need any help from you!"

"I wish I could, kid, but I'm pretty sure we're stuck with each other."

I quickened my pace and grumbled, thinking I needed to see Dr. Hitchfield right away. Explain to him my worries about Mother, my longing about my father—he loves that—and then let it slip out with three minutes left in our fifty-minute hour, 'Oh, by the way, I've been talking to a ghost who claims to be my father.' His blue eyes would squint, just noticeable if you were watching closely, and then he would check the knot on his tie before asking about my appetite, sleep, and work. It would be a test. Would he increase my Prozac, give me something for hallucinations, keep me over my hour, or would he have me hospitalized? It would be fun to see what Hitchfield would do, but I couldn't afford a few days on a psych unit. I'd tell him everything except Max.

No, if I'm cracking up, then I had better get the help I needed before I was completely out of touch. Elizabeth would take care of Mother. Yes, I'd lay it all out for Hitchfield. How would Mother take it?

I stopped walking for a moment and blurted, "My mother is going to die. It will be the best thing for her. It's something I've wanted for a while. But I wish it could be different. I feel guilty about fantasizing about having her killed. And now this!"

"Look, from what I saw, you should get a medal."

"From a guy who ran out on his pregnant girlfriend? Hmm, that really doesn't mean much."

"Ouch. I understand—I'm a toad looking for the princess."

"You're supposed to be here to help me. Do you think you can be serious?"

"Sure, relax. What does she need?"

"A new heart and a pair of lungs." My voice cracked.

"Can't they do a transplant?"

"She was a candidate until a few years ago." I shook my head. "Now she's too weak; she'd never survive the operation." As I said it, a man in his forties came out of DiMaggio's Bakery, makers of the best cannoli in the world. The man had two brown bakery boxes in one hand and a loaf of bread in the other. Our eyes met, and he gave me a quick once-over. I gave him a sheepish grin, and he returned a look of consternation. I quickened my pace. Thankfully he went straight to his car, a few feet from us.

"Hey, Rodney, you're going to blow this thing if you keep talking to me. You should pretend you're talking on your phone."

It was a good idea, but I was in no mood to take advice from Max. I looked in every direction before saying through my teeth, "Just take off."

"I can't, and your moaning about it is getting old. I've been sent. After the fan crushed my skull, I didn't say, 'Hey, maybe I should swing by and see my son. So let's try to work together because I think that's what's supposed to happen. I'm supposed to help you."

"Pleeease, don't say you're here to help me anymore. I can't function like this, with you at my elbow. Mother thinks I've gone bananas. She's worried about me trying to kill her, and it's all because of you!"

"You keep yapping, and people will think you're a psycho. A well-dressed psycho, but most people are more concerned about how crazy you are than about the expensive threads. That suit, a lightweight tweed—it's nice. English?" I nodded. "And those shoes look softer than ballet slippers. Italian?" I nodded. "I got an idea. Until we get to your work, I'll talk, and you blink for a no and nod for yes."

"Maybe we should just walk and enjoy the day," I said. We crossed Hartford Street and moved from my working-class neighborhood made up mostly of three-family homes, with the owner living on the first floor, to a wedge of despair between my cozy neighborhood and the downtown business district where Haynesworth's was located.

"This neighborhood, it's the kind of place you lock your doors in the daytime and never walk around alone. Yet, here you are trying to save the planet by walking through a place that scares the dead," Max said as we passed Briscoe's Ribs and Chicken Shack, Hombre's Bar, and the Calypso Liquid Store.

"The food pantry is just up the street," I said, as if explaining the presence of a toothless woman with thinning white hair sitting on the pavement in front of the liquor store. She gawked at me with her good eye; the other looked like glass. Before we passed her, she groaned, "Can you spare some change?" An arthritic hand jutted out toward me.

I stopped and handed her two dollars.

"God bless," she said.

"Why don't you just go buy her a bottle?" Max said.

"You wouldn't understand."

"Keep talking, and you'll be explaining yourself first to a cop and then to a counselor on a locked psych ward. You'll be trading that English tweed for a hospital johnny."

"All right, a blink for no," I muttered.

"So what do you do for excitement?"

"Blink for no?"

"Take it easy. You don't have to take my head off. Let me think."

I marched on with strident steps, trying to show my frustration and anger. That's when it hit me—I was really nuts. Only a madman would have conversations with an imaginary father. How great are my delusions, concocting the whole ghost-of-father-coming-to-help-me thing?

"Okay, I got one. You've got no friends?"

"I will not answer." I repeated this over and over to myself and kept walking, ignoring Max, who kept pace with me. "It is insane to talk to a ghost because ghosts do not exist. And unless you're five, you're too old to talk to imaginary people. I won't say another word."

"Okay, Rodney, maybe I should have phrased that more gently. Can I call you Rod?"

I kept walking, face straight ahead, telling myself, "I will not answer; ghosts do not exist."

"I like Rod much more than Rodney. I think Rod, and I think of hunting and fishing. I think strength, you know, a powerful rod, a big stick, a man's man. I hear Rodney, and I see guys like you, no girlfriend and afraid of their mother. From now on it's Rod and Max." I glared at him, and he said pleadingly, "It's a start."

I started running, telling myself, "He isn't real."

"You late? Where's the fire?"

I put my head down and barreled forward.

"What the hell, are you late?" Max asked, staying right alongside of me. I sped up and felt a pain in my side and throat. But there he was, effortlessly matching me step for step. I slowed down just a bit, and Max automatically dropped down a gear. After a block my soft, out-of-shape body protested more vigorously. My sides felt as if a hand had reached inside me and squeezed my lungs. I slowed down a bit more and realized that the questions he asked were logical. If he were a hallucination, wouldn't he be telling me to kill myself or kill my mother or the president, or telling me things like I'm stupid or that Martians would be landing soon and they wanted to move in with me and Mother? Shit, he's just asking me if I'm late because I'm running; that makes perfect sense.

"No, I'm not late," I snapped.

"I tell you, Rod you keep talking to me, you're going to get in trouble, big-time trouble. All it takes is one wrong person seeing you arguing with yourself."

I stopped and yelled, "Are you a hallucination?"

"All's I know is I died and found myself in your kitchen. The tragic end of Maxwell Dowling was no hallucination."

"I feel like I'm going crazy."

"Relax; I'm here with you. This has got to be something special. I say, let's make the most of it, just relax, and go with it."

"That's your advice?" I screamed and turned—bang—right into a tall black woman who was coming out of Dunkin' Donuts. In my Max-induced rage, arms flailing, head feeling as if it were going to explode, I knocked her drink out of her hand. The cover popped off, and the container's contents, a cold, caramel-brown liquid, splashed full force onto my lap. My first impression, given the neighborhood and her appearance, was that she was a prostitute. She was wearing a gold micromini and matching six-inch heeled boots that kissed the bottom of her knees. She had scary, long, gold-painted nails, green eye shadow, and hoop earrings that would work better as bracelets. She was accompanied by a short, thin, blond young man in a tight-fitting red satin shirt and snow-white jeans. He looked like he had long been denied sunlight.

"Shit, man!" the woman yelled, and heaved the rest of her drink in the air as if I needed a hazelnut-frozen-coffee shower. The beverage caught the right side of my face and chest. Copious portions of the monastic-brown liquid landed on my jacket and merged with my already drenched pants, leaving me with the I-just-wet-my-pants look.

"Where the hell are you going, Charlie Brown!" the woman yelled.

"I'm so sorry," I said, bending over to retrieve her cup. In that moment I knew she was more than I could handle. But rather than being intimidated, I found myself drawn to her voice.

"Who the hell were you screaming at?" she demanded, hands on hips.

For a moment she looked like the most beautiful woman in the world. I turned away out of fear of what

I might do as part of me very much wanted to wrap my arms around her in the hope of receiving a warm embrace in return. My eyes locked onto her companion, who gave me a seductive wink. Impulsively, I winked back. I was both repulsed and drawn. I thought, rather than seeing what the rest of the day will bring, maybe killing myself right now is my best option. I quickly diverted my eyes away from him and pulled out my handkerchief and began wiping my soaked pants. A small puddle had gathered in my shoe, settling under the arch of my right foot. I knew the chance of my handkerchief making a difference was remote, but watching the stain darken on my suit as I dabbed away was preferable to looking at this pair of urban troubles that I found incredibly frightfully attractive. The woman threw me side glances as I brushed more furiously with my hankie. Each glance of her raised a chorus of condemnation from somewhere in my psyche that said, "She's a hooker; you need to leave."

"I said who the hell were you yelling at, Mr. Thousand-Dollar-Suits, strutting down Dog Turd Avenue like you own the place?"

"No one."

"Shit, man, you were tearing into someone," she said. Her blond friend smiled, made the international sign for crazy, and again winked. For some unknown reason, I took this as him being sympathetic.

"You did it now," Max said. "They're hookers; yell police, and they'll screw down the shit hole they popped out of. Yell it, man—the police are the friend of white men in thousand-dollar suits, especially when they're getting jammed up by Long Tall Sally and her sweet, little, fried-brained friend."

"What you going to say for yourself?" she asked with authority.

"I'm sorry," I said, meekly trying to avoid eye contact but feeling overwhelmed by her sharp, roughly feminine voice, which I found sexually arousing. "Let me buy you another drink," I said, and smiled, thinking I could listen to her all day long, never mind her companion, who smelled like a field of lilacs.

"Sure, but that's a large hazelnut frozen coffee."

I nodded, afraid to look at this amazingly beautiful woman and her anemic buddy. The stain on my pants started off strong along the inner thigh and then formed a trickle running down to my ankle. I knew I wanted to know her better, but she intimidated me, paralyzed me with fear. I remembered what Dr. Hitchfield had told me once when summarizing my vague occasional homicidal wishes toward Mother: it is bad, but until you act upon it, all you've done is undermine your sense of self. I might find myself aroused at the sight of a black hooker in a micro-mini and her male associate, but as long as I buried those thoughts and never came this way again, what harm was there?

"You want to buy me a coffee, fine, but who were you yelling at?"

"Don't be an idiot," Max hollered, "Scream police like your life depended on it!"

"I got problems at work. I took a friend's advice, and it was the worst thing I could have done. I was practicing how I was going to blast him." I found myself staring at the top of her gold boots, not her knees, just the gold vinyl. It felt safer.

"You want to have a little fun, forget work?" she said. I looked up at her both horrified and tempted. She gave a mischievous smile, and I was ready to go anywhere with her. "I can turn your blues into New Year's Eve and the Fourth of July all rolled into one for two hundred."

A deep fear seized me. I shook my head and shifted my eyes back to her boots.

"I think he's more interested in what I can offer," the young man said.

I gulped and imagined myself in bed with the two of them. A cold sweat covered me from my neck to my backside.

"Where do you work?" she asked.

"Haynesworth and Waite's."

"My, my, isn't that sweet? You sure do dress the part," she cooed, playing with my lapels.

"Let me buy you a drink," I said, pulling away. Her mention of money sank in and chilled me. What's happening to me? Dr. Hitchfield, who had the physique and complexion of a bamboo shoot, flashed before me.

Emergency session, perhaps daily for the next week or two, I thought.

"Drink!" Max shouted.

"Coffee," I corrected myself.

"Beatrice, Dinky, who you playing with," snarled a man who had come up from behind them. His head was shaven, and he sported several days of beard, which darkened his grimy white face. He was in his thirties, my height, muscular. His eyes were hard and crazed, a mix of anger and confusion. Under his pale-orange cashmere sweater, I imagined a wiry guy with coconuts for biceps and granite abs.

"Spike, this dude walked into me, spilled my coffee," Beatrice said.

I looked at him and thought, Yes, Spike. A man who could drive his fists through me as if I were cotton candy.

"You messing with my ladies?" Spike wrinkled his nose disapprovingly.

"Police, police, police, police..." Max sang with increasing alarm.

"It was an accident, and I was just about to buy—Beatrice, is it?—another drink." Maybe Max was right, but with Spike's interruption, I felt less sexually aroused. I guess fear has a way of doing that.

"For fifty, I can play your fiddle for a while," Beatrice said, smiling and making a motion with her fingers as if playing a piano.

"Maybe you need to show me the macho man in you," Dinky said.

My legs trembled. "No, I couldn't, I've got to get to work," I said as we entered the coffee shop. I took a deep breath. Shit, it sounded inviting though. "Beatrice, that's nice, you don't hear that name too much these days." I was relieved. I found myself fixed on her butt. It was a relief—it was a nice, firm butt, but it wasn't exactly sexually interesting. Better to focus on a woman's bum than on a boy's tantalizing aroma. Beatrice had a striking presence that on first look had reminded me of a black super model. Would there be anything wrong with desiring a super model? I felt like I had just taken a step away from the edge. My breathing was approaching normal. I commanded myself to never address Dinky, not a look or word.

"It was my mother's name. Good woman. She saved me; without her I'd either be in the nuthouse or dead. She died when I was fifteen, them's the breaks."

"You don't make small talk with these kinds of people," Max whispered. I know ghosts don't sweat, but I imagined beads building on his quivering upper lip.

I was intoxicated with Beatrice's voice and the sweet scent of Dinky but equally frightened by the reality of buying a prostitute her morning coffee. I thought of Dr. Hitchfield tilting his head the way he often did when he was about to say, "Interesting." I gulped air desperately, searched for something to say, and mumbled, "My mother has had the opposite effect on me."

"What, your mommy didn't love you?" Beatrice said in a whiny voice.

"This is suicide!" Max yelled, and turned away as if expecting something awful.

"Let's just say she's a hard person to live with."

"What the hell are you doing still living with your mother?" Spike laughed. "My girl's time is money. You understand?"

I felt a definite threat.

"Spike, what we got here is a big shot who's set up over at that swank-assed Haynesworth and Waite's," Beatrice said.

"What else do you know about him?" Spike posed, again in a threatening way. "All's I see is you wasting time unless you two walk out of here *together!*"

"Spike!" Beatrice hollered.

"You don't ever do that," Spike snapped at her, and then turned back to me and in a slightly calmer tone, asked, "So you got some pull over at Haynesworth's?"

"I'm a salesman."

"You take care of a friend?" Spike asked, poking my ribs.

"Get your skinny white ass out of here," Max yelled, his eyes about to pop through his Batman mask.

"We have a preferred-customer plan, ten percent off on sales over a thousand."

"Maybe you can set me up with a white suit, three-piece. Something classy that lets you-all know Spike is here." Spike ran his hands down his sides as if proud of himself.

"Police fucked up my white suit. That's how the world knows Spike. It's my trademark."

"Yes, I think we have some wonderful Caribbean items left over from the summer. You a forty-two regular?" I gulped.

"You can hook me up?" Spike asked, slapping my back hard. He made a face that sent an express message to my brain's fear center: "I'm a badass, and I can hurt you."

I smiled nervously and pretended I hadn't heard him.

Two customers ahead of us got their orders and left.

I turned to Beatrice, and she ordered from the young Woman behind the counter, "Another frozen coffee you know how Bea-bop likes it." Beatrice tapped her long nails seductively on the countertop, and I imagined her bringing me great pleasure. For a second, I considered running away with her.

"You want anything?" I said, looking at Spike.

"No, I'm cool. You know, you dress the bomb. I like a man who has an eye for threads. Love that Haynesworth look." He raised an eyebrow and gave me a quick salute.

"Thanks."

"What's your name?" Spike asked.

"Rodney." As it came out, a petrified little voice inside me said, "Don't tell him."

"You are about to get ripped off," Max yelled.

"Rodney, I like the finer things," Spike said. He then winked and asked in a sly voice, "You like my little boy, Dinky?"

Dinky half closed his eyes and blew me a kiss.

He looked very desirable. I had to fight back an urge to wink. "No, no, no," I said, and quickly turned my attention back to the salesclerk, giving her five dollars and telling her to keep the change. I nodded a goodbye to Beatrice and Spike, avoiding Dinky's gaze as if additional contact would be hazardous to my health.

"Get your ass out of here before you get shot or arrested," Max yelled.

"You got sweet eyes," Beatrice said, tapping my shoulder.

I nodded, feeling helpless.

"Rod, seriously, this is how people get killed," Max said.

I nodded again.

"Hey, if you change your mind, I work Washington Street, down by Good-Time Charlie's Café, from sunset to whenever." As Beatrice spoke, my yearning for her grew.

"Hey, take that shit outside," the stocky Dunkin' Donuts manager barked.

Beatrice smiled and flicked a quick goodbye wave.

"Get out of here!" the manager yelled, and embarrassingly I was the only one to jump.

We all headed for the door.

As I pushed open the door, Beatrice smiled warmly and said, "Good-Time Charlie's. I can make it a great time." Spike looked as if he had a serious attack of indigestion.

"I'll remember that, thanks," I said as we parted ways.

I could hear Spike yelling at her—something about be professional, or he'd fix her pretty black ass.

CHAPTER 5

FATHER'S ADVICE

Max and I agreed to stop talking until we reached Haynesworth and Waite's. Because of my Beatrice detour, I felt pushed to pick up the pace the rest of the way. As we moved, the world gradually shifted from decaying tenements and shabby storefronts to towering office buildings with elegant street-level businesses and upscale stores occupying smaller edifices. Beatrice's spill continued to be uncomfortably wet on my inner right thigh. I banked on getting to work before anyone else and changing into some dressy, off-the-rack pants with a reasonably well-matched sport coat. The way my day was going, I was relieved as we approached Haynesworth's to see the store's locked security gate in place.

As I unlocked the gate and pushed it to the far left of the store's entry, Max said, "They trust you with the keys?"

I nodded and moved to the front door, fumbling for a second to find the right key.

"I'm impressed." Max paused as we entered, and then he howled, "This is a goldmine! Are they treating you right?"

I locked the door behind us and headed toward the dress slacks.

"I said, 'Are they treating you right?'"

"Yes," I said, trying to sound bored as I perused thirty-two-by-thirty-inch pants.

"Because you know, if they're not, they're crazy. See, they trust you with the keys, and you've been here awhile; you could, if you used your head, rob them blind."

"Is that helping me?"

Max quickly shifted his eyes as if readying for a giant cat to pounce on him and meekly said, "Sorry."

I grabbed a pair of charcoal-gray trousers and then a lighter gray jacket and headed for the dressing room, where I flipped off my shoes and carefully hung my stained pants, trying my best to prevent wrinkles.

"By the way, what the hell were you thinking of back there?" Max said.

"Look, I got a lot on my mind," I said as I slipped on the new pants. Good fit, I thought, checking myself out in the full-length mirror. I glanced over my left shoulder at Max, who was surprisingly absent from the mirror.

"I can't believe it, you were talking like you're some kind of long-lost buddy to those two sewer rats.

Guaranteed they're oozing with the creeping crud. And one look at that asshole in the orange sweater anyone with half a brain would have walked, no run away."

"Spike?"

"Spike, yeah, with a face only a mother could love. He's the first person I've ever seen in the flesh with two gold teeth."

"Gold teeth?"

"Yeah, his incisors. That Beatrice must be working hard." Max sighed. "You know, you were running a big risk talking to those losers. You never know if the police are watching. They see a young white guy dressed like a million, they got to figure you're buying services. That was mistake number one. Mistake number two, you know clowns like that trio are notorious for robbing squares like you. They make a deal—cheap blow job, whatever—then they take you someplace out of sight, and you end up missing a wallet, watch, and maybe your pants."

"How's this look?" I asked as I put the jacket on.

"You didn't hear a word I said," Max protested.

"I need to make an important call," I said as I stepped into my shoes.

"Go ahead."

"It's personal," I said, opening the dressing room door.

"Well, excuse me. But sorry, I get a front-row seat to the wonderful world of Rodney." I grimaced, and Max said confidentially, "What are you worried about? It's not like I can tell anyone but you what I hear."

"It's to my therapist, and I'd feel better if you weren't around."

"And I'd feel better if I got a call from St. Peter apologizing for my little detour into Rodney World, but baby, until that happens, we're stuck with each other."

"Can't you just wait here, and I'll call from the front desk?"

"I don't control it. You go there," Max said, pointing to the front of the store, "and I'm as certain as water is wet that I'll be right by your side." He smiled and shrugged.

"Try."

"What the hell. Go on, Rod; I'll hang here," Max said, grabbing onto a table of men's dress shirts that started at ninety-five dollars.

"Okay," I said, and backed away from him. On my third step, he was magically standing next to me looking like he had had an encounter with the giant cat.

"What?"

"The sexy voice told me to follow directions and listen. It's very important to the both of us for me to pay attention." Max raised his arms as if surrendering.

"You look scared."

"It's like you're inside the voice. Like the voice is a fireworks grand finale, and you're in the middle of it. Looks like I'm with you, and there's no getting around it."

I frowned. "She said, 'Listen'?"

"Right. I guess she doesn't want me screwing around. Why the hell do you have to call a therapist anyways?"

"For starters, I see you."

"You tell a shrink you're seeing dead people, talking to them, he'll be on the horn to the police, and you'll be in a padded cell quicker than Beatrice can give head."

"Well, yeah, then there's that little encounter."

"What?"

"With Beatrice and Dinky," I said, and nervously began buttoning and unbuttoning my jacket.

"What, do you have to report every time something weird happens?"

"No, but I think this was significant."

"Significant. If anyone back there needs a shrink, it was that trio of losers."

"Sometimes there's more going on than meets the eye."

"So what's the big deal that I missed?" Max asked, spreading out his arms and then quickly folding them on his chest.

"You wouldn't understand."

"Give it a whirl. Just think, you might be the one and only person to get advice from the other side. You play this right, you could be on all the talk shows, maybe get your own show Rod Armstrong, mystic, the man who traveled to the other side, a man of mystery and mysterious ways, va-va-voom."

"Can't you be serious?" I snapped.

"Sure I could, but you're serious enough for the both of us."

I sucked on my bottom lip.

"Okay, don't start crying. I'll be totally serious. What is it that's so important you need to run over and see a shrink about?"

"No offense, but you seem to be a less-than-sensitive guy."

Max looked me up and down. He shook his head and said, "What the hell does sensitive have to do with anything? We're two men." Max looked me in the eye and gave an agonizing "Oh no."

"What?"

"You're thinking of seeing that freak Beatrice."

"Well."

"Well, what?"

"This is very difficult."

"Give it a shot. I may be dead, but I've had sex with just about every kind of woman there is and found myself liking it more the older I got." Max gave a satisfied sigh.

"It just would be better if I talked with Dr. Hitchfield."

"You don't get it. You go see your doctor" he said *doctor* in an it's-a-waste-of-time way. "I'm there right with you, buddy. You're on the couch, and I might end up behind the good doctor making goofy faces. So wouldn't it be better if you ran it by me first?"

"You have to remember your showing up has been a major stressor."

"Please, cry me a river; see what suddenly getting your head crushed and dying does to your stress levels."

I looked around and then my eyes sheepishly landed on the floor in front of me as I mumbled, "I found Beatrice attractive."

"You found *that* attractive? No, what was attractive was a woman wriggling around in a gold kerchief for a skirt. It was attractive because you are sex starved, pure and simple. Rodney, you need to find a girl."

I gave a slight nod and said, "I also found Dinky attractive."

Max turned away from me and looked up at the ceiling and moaned, "This can't really be my kid."

"You wanted to know."

"You can't be serious."

I crossed my arms and said, "Afraid so."

"Let's you and me go nightclubbing tonight."

"I don't think so. But before other people get here, I'm calling Dr. Hitchfield."

Max knowingly shook his head. "You ever have sex with a man?"

"No!"

"You ever have sex with a little boy?"

"No!"

"Good. You ever have sex with a lady?"

I paused, and Max coaxed me with sympathetic eyes. "No," I whispered.

"What you need is a girl. Ideally not a hooker, but if that's where we start, so be it."

"What I need is to talk to someone I trust about all of this."

"A friend?"

I sighed.

"Yes, you need a girl and a friend." Max rubbed his chin and said, "You need to start living, kid."

"I am."

"No, you're existing. First, what exactly happened with Beatrice and Dinky?"

"Don't laugh."

Max nodded.

"She looked like the sexiest woman alive. He smelled great, and her voice drove me wild." Then my voice rose and raced as if I were both devastated and scared. "I would have done anything and everything with them."

"The important thing is, you did nothing with them. Anything like this happen before?"

"No."

"You're thirty-five?"

I nodded.

"You got any fantasies?"

"That's none of your business."

"Tell me, what is your dream date? What does she look like?"

"I don't know."

"Come on, every guy knows what really turns him on, so what is it, Rod?"

"Okay, I'd say the classic beauties, innocent, not too aggressive."

"Good, so you like the sweet girls, nothing like Beatrice."

"But those are an ideal, an abstraction. When faced with a male and a female hooker, I'm so aroused. I'm surprised I didn't take them up on their offer."

"Sex is an escape from stress. Here you are, sex starved your entire life."

I frowned.

"What? Am I right or what?"

I grudgingly nodded.

"No friends, worried about when will your crab apple mother kick off, and presto, in drops the father you've never known, but he's a ghost. So Beatrice and stinky Dinky come by like a neon sign flashing, 'Sex sale: all welcomed—straights, gays, kinky whatevers, we got a deal for you,' and you want to be first in line."

I gently shook my head.

"You need to start meeting girls."

"When I'm getting aroused by a man, your advice is to start seeing girls?"

"Of course. If you were overweight and had a bad ticker, I'd be telling you to get off your ass and exercise. It's the same."

"Huh?"

"Look, there are reasons why you wanted to get it on with them. They may be sick reasons, but they are there.

All you have to do is provide the cash, and for a half hour or whatever, they will take care of you. You have needs, and for a few minutes, they can make you feel like they're filling those needs. What led you to this condition is a life without knowing women. The remedy is simple."

"I'm not going to see a prostitute."

"I didn't think you would. It's not a bad idea as long as you're protected. But I was thinking, are there any other girls in your life, neighbors, co-workers?"

I paused, hesitating to mention Lana Sayers, the front-counter cashier, beautiful Lana, whom I've been thinking of asking out for over three years and whom I've discussed with Dr. Hitchfield on numerous occasions.

"Come on, Rod; there must be somebody."

"Yes, I've been thinking about asking Lana out," I whispered, as if afraid my secret would reverberate through the store forever and ever.

"Who's Lana?"

I walked over to a display of sweaters and began straightening them. I was trying to act like Lana was no big deal when the truth was, I wished more than anything to be with her and had grown to see her as possibly my best chance at ever being with a woman. "She's the cashier at the front desk. She handles all sales once they are final."

"She's the checkout girl because this place is too fancy for you to ring up the sales, get your hands dirty taking in the dough that pays the bills and keeps you in your fancy suits. Crazy, crazy, crazy."

"It's the way Haynesworth and Waite's is; I didn't create the system. I just work here."

"Yeah, yeah. So what's Lana like?"

"She's wonderful. She lives with her mother and raises angelfish. Her father was killed in a horrible accident, but he was found negligent, and the family got nothing from the insurance."

Max interrupted me. "Oh yes, this is a match made in heaven. I can see it now—she's scraping algae off aquarium walls while you're poring over letters from some rebel soldier who died over a hundred years ago."

"See, that's why I didn't want to talk to you about my feelings."

"You've spent too much time with Dr. Hitchfield and not enough time making a move on Lana. It's simple."

I shook my head but privately thought Max might be right.

"What does Lana look like?"

"She's beautiful. Blond hair, cut short but feminine; blue eyes; slim, youthful body."

"You got this gorgeous thing here, and you haven't asked her out?"

"It's complicated."

"Everything is complicated if you make it complicated. Sometimes once you jump into it, you find out complicated is a piece of cake."

"We're friends. She gives me rides home if I've walked and the weather turns bad."

"Good," Max said, rubbing his hands together as if relishing thoughts of me and Lana.

"I listen to her problems about her mother, who has as many health problems as my mother. She's the most caring person imaginable. She helps me from going completely nuts with Mother, the job, everything. She understands how hard it is."

"You got the perfect setup."

"You make it sound dirty."

"It's good to have fun, Rod. So what are you going to do?"

"Talk with Dr. Hitchfield about all of it: Beatrice, Dinky, Lana, Mother. I need him."

"You need Lana, or someone like her. End of story. I tell you, if I were you, I'd stop seeing the shrink and start seeing Lana. Give that a week, and you'll be smiling a lot more. Give it a month, and the Civil War will start being something you used to care about."

I pulled out my cell phone and punched in Dr. Hitchfield's number. There was an opening at two o'clock. I repeatedly thanked Eleanor, the receptionist.

"My word, you'd think you hit the lottery," Max teased.

"You don't understand how busy he is."

"Now, Lana I can't wait to meet."

"I wish you were gone."

"Me too."

"You know, you were told to listen. Maybe you need to start doing more of that."

"Whatever. All's I know is when you're doing something stupid, acting in ways that are going to hurt you, I'm obligated to say something."

"That's your opinion."

The front door opened, and Mr. Duncan Waite, great-great-great-grandson of Norbert Waite, co-founder with Chester Haynesworth, of the business, entered. "Rodney, Rodney, are you back there?" Mr. Waite locked the door behind him. There were still a few minutes before opening.

"Yes, Mr. Waite."

"The owner?" Max asked.

I nodded.

"Shit, he looks like a cross between a pumpkin and Dracula."

"Sh."

"He can't hear me. I bet he dyes that mop. Must use his wife's stuff because that shade of orange is something you don't find in nature, and you never find it on men." As Mr. Waite got closer, Max started laughing and said, "Any more face lifts, he'll cut himself sneezing."

Mr. Waite carried a coffee container in his right hand and had a rolled-up morning newspaper lodged under his armpit. We met in the center of the store. I always felt like a five-year-old when alone with him.

"Rodney, today I need you to take stock of our gloves, scarves, hats, and sweaters. Christmas will be here before you know it, and I want to make sure we're set on all those impulse items that girlfriends and wives will be looking to stuff stockings with. I'll be in my office if you need me. Anyone else here?"

"No."

"That jacket really doesn't go with those trousers."

"Yes, I was in a hurry this morning."

"Something that gives more contrast would work better."

Max, looking like he would explode, said, "You get in early, and there's not a thank-you? Oh no, there's a critique of what you're wearing."

"I think you're right," I said to Mr. Waite.

Mr. Waite started toward his office.

"Oh, sir? I have a nasty toothache and made an appointment with my dentist for two o'clock."

"Toothache? Really?"

"Sensitive to hot and cold," I said.

"I had that problem not so long ago, put my tongue over the tooth whenever I ate or drank."

"Is it still bothering you?"

"Oh no, got it fixed the next day."

"Nice job, Rod," Max said, and gave me a thumbs-up.

Mr. Waite pursed his lips and then said, "So you want your lunch at two. Fine, work it out with Van."

There was a rapping at the front door. I guessed it would be Lana. I usually arrived about half an hour early, followed by Mr. Waite ten minutes before opening, and then Lana a few minutes before the other salesmen,

Van Paxton and Simon Parretti, who usually strolled in just as we were about to open.

I excused myself, and Mr. Waite left for his office, where he typically spent the morning reading the newspaper and phoning friends.

"Sonny boy, if I wasn't dead, I'd be getting her number," Max said, staring at Lana as she came through the front door. I fought back the urge to hit him.

Max giggled and said, "One could do far worse."

CHAPTER 6

WHEN SAUSAGE DOGS MEET GHOSTS

After exchanging pleasantries, Lana and I assumed our normal work positions. She stood with a welcoming smile at the front counter, wearing a pale-green knit top and matching skirt that fell an inch below her knees. Van Paxton, store manager, was at the back of the store, ten feet from the boss's office, prepared to jump to Mr. Waite's assistance. Van, a tall, thin man in his late fifties, prided himself on the speed of his tennis serve. He had spent his life measuring inseams, straightening shoulders, and for the last five years, avoiding customers. Alone at the back of the store, he had a knack of fading into the merchandise as if on a secret clothier mission that required camouflage. He was Mr. Waite's eyes and ears, with loyalties to self and boss, in that order. Van had broken me into the Haynesworth and Waite world as he had Simon six years prior to my coming on board.

Simon, in his mid-forties, was working on his third marriage. He was a chameleon, able to change his views, even personality, in midsentence if he thought a sale was in jeopardy. Simon spent his mornings pretending to sort shirts: his real purpose, though, was to entertain Van as they waited for business to pick up. Between girlfriends and ex-wives, Simon and Van had plenty to talk about.

Being the junior sales associate, the expectation was that I would work from the time I opened the store to when it closed. I always caught the first customer to walk in, with Simon picking up the next if I was still attending to a sale. If three or four customers came our way, Simon and I would rove about among them. Van's rule was that he was only needed if five or more customers happened upon us at the same time. Since this seldom happened, Van had an incredibly good thing going.

Armed with a clipboard, inventory lists, and pen, I began taking count of our gloves. Behind sliding doors under the display case were boxes of leather and suede gloves of assorted sizes, styles, and colors. On my knees, I pulled up a box of extra-large, fur-lined, chocolate-colored gloves.

"What gives with those two jokers?" Max asked.

I looked up with my index finger pressed to my lips.

"They won't hear you unless you start yelling again," Max said confidentially.

I stood and placed the box of gloves on the display case, choosing to ignore him.

"So you're the odd man out."

"What do you mean?" I whispered.

"I mean, they're polluting the place with wild tales of how lover boy," Max said, rolling his eyes, "has won the heart and body of a future Miss America. And you're crawling around on your knees counting gloves."

"I don't mind."

"Of course you do; don't give me that line of bull." Max paused, waiting for my response, which I wasn't ready to offer. "You should do a slowdown. You know, do everything in slow motion. When the boss wants to know how come things aren't done, you just look over at those two. End of story."

"Look, I got things to do here." I bent down and picked up another box of gloves.

"You know, you're a tough guy to help," Max said. He looked up at the ceiling and said softly, "I hope you guys are paying attention to what's going on here."

Playing in the background was Beethoven's *Pastoral* Symphony. It stopped for a second, announcing that the front door had opened. I could hear Lana's greeting. "Good morning what a beautiful day." I looked at my watch. I would give the customer thirty seconds to run her or his eyes around the place. It was enough time to give him or her the opportunity to move toward any items of interest, enough time to run out if a few price tags provided a startle but not so long to make them feel ignored and start wondering if Haynesworth and Waite's high standards of customer service were a thing of the past.

I turned toward the front entrance and there, standing across from the beautiful, soft-spoken Lana was the exceptionally bubbly and wealthy Mrs. Beverly Buffington, formerly Miss Beverly Milton, whose family made a fortunate in banking and railroads after the Civil War. Mrs. Buffington was a strange-looking woman of sixty whose chin had been swallowed by her neck and whose nose, the most distinguishing feature on her heavily painted face, was larger than her pet sausage dog's head. The tiny dog, Caesar by name, was sandwiched between her enormous breasts and flabby right forearm.

As I approached, I heard Mrs. Buffington gushing to Lana, "My nephew, Ethan, marvelous boy, is spending Thanksgiving with us. He's a freshman at Williams, and rather than fly home, he decided to spend the holiday with us."

"Good morning, Mrs. Buffington."

"Oh, Rodney, so glad you're here today. I was just saying how my nephew, Ethan, is spending the holiday with Roy and me, and I wanted to get him something special. It's not too often we have the attention of the younger generation, so I do want everything to be just right." Caesar began wiggling desperately. His little mouth showed a row of sharp teeth. His eyes bulged, making me think Mrs. Buffington's flab might have collapsed the dachshund's lungs.

"Now you be a good boy," Mrs. Buffington said, snuggling the animal up closer to her cheek. Caesar growled.

"I think he can see me," Max said.

My eyes widened as dry mouth and panic began setting in. I stepped back.

Caesar barked three times in Max's direction. Each bark grew in strength. Max stepped back as far from me as he could, which was only an arm's length, and angled himself between Caesar and me.

"Hush, hush, my little precious," Mrs. Buffington said, positioning Caesar a bit lower in her arm and tightening her grasp on the pooch. The poor little dog's eyes betrayed the strain it was under. If she had squeezed just a little more, I'm sure his eyes would have shot out of their sockets. He howled and snapped at Max.

"I can't believe this," Max said.

I gave the dog a weak smile, attempting to communicate that all was well. Apparently, Mrs. Buffington interpreted my expression as fear because she said in a very soothing voice, "Now don't worry; my little baby doesn't bite." She then shoved Caesar under my nose. He growled and clawed the air with his tiny front paws.

"Shit, he definitely sees me," Max said. "Definitely. You got to get out of here."

I gulped and took another step back. My stomach went from feeling a tad uneasy to becoming a mighty rumbling mess.

"No kidding, Rodney, the little mutt sees me."

Max's panic, thankfully, seemed to steady me a bit.

"Oh, dear, dear Rodney, don't be frightened." Mrs. Buffington stepped forward with Caesar barking and flailing his small front paws. "You're scaring him now. He's picking up your jitters and thinks you're about to attack. He's very sensitive. He's recovering from a nasty intestinal virus. His first day out."

Max started to regain his nerve, and he stuck his head around my shoulder and leaned forward into Caesar's little face. Max made a kissing sound and, for some inexplicable reason, let out a bloodcurdling growl. In response, Caesar let loose a howl that would have done wild wolves proud. I jumped toward Mrs. Buffington, which scared her and caused her to lose hold of her four-legged baby. Caesar, in midair, looked as if he had been electrocuted. His tail, ears, and legs all stiffened for a moment as he flew by Max, who suddenly became frightened again and dropped to his knees, trying to hide behind Mrs. Buffington, who screamed after Caesar, who had turned into a reddish-brown blur racing away from her.

Max took a deep breath and said, "Cat. I was in its paws for a second. I thought I was a goner."

"You're dead," I whispered through clenched jaw as I chased after Mrs. Buffington.

What Caesar lacked in size, he made up for in determination as he sprinted down a narrow aisle with men's suits on the right and pants on the left. Mrs. Buffington, on the other hand, could not get her legs into second gear. She made impassioned thrusts with her arms and shoulders as if hoping her upper limbs would aid in her pursuit of the speedy Caesar. As she huffed and puffed forward, she repeatedly pled with the dog. "Come here. Be a good boy."

Mrs. Buffington maintained a course down the middle of the aisle, preventing me from passing her. Fortunately, I could see around her enough to keep track of Caesar's route. Max, behind me, kept apologizing, saying. "Sorry. I guess they haven't worked out the whole dog thing. You'd think they'd make us dog proof. Wonder what else can see me."

The sight of Beverly Buffington lumbering through the store, with me side-straddling behind her looking for an opportunity to pass, got Simon's attention as we headed for the glove display.

"What's going on?" Simon shouted, sounding irritated and looking at me as if I were to blame for this totally un–Haynesworth and Waite's behavior. Due to Caesar's diminutive stature, Simon didn't see him as he darted between the salesman's legs.

"What's the problem?" Simon demanded again.

"Loose dog," I said, and pointed with my eyes and head to the floor behind him.

Simon turned as Caesar let out a yelp and hurried inside the cabinet that stored our supply of gloves.

"You should have closed that door," Max said. I gave him a quick dirty look, and he backed off by saying, "At least you got him cornered."

"I'm allergic to dogs," Simon said, and retreated several feet away from Mrs. Buffington, whose overexertion had moistened her makeup and given her a spooky wax-figure look.

I looked across at Van Paxton, who remained at his station, punching away at his day planner, acting as if nothing was happening.

"Caesar, Mommy has a goody for her little precious." Mrs. Buffington, bending at the waist, held a cinnamon-colored dog biscuit a few inches from the open cabinet door. "Come to Mama, my baby," she repeated, gradually increasing her tempo and delivering the five words in a consistent rhythm, which were punctuated in a timely fashion by Caesar's forlorn yelps. I prayed for patience.

A break in Beethoven's Sixth let us know another customer had entered the store. Simon quickly left us for what I imagined he thought would be far more predictable interactions than what might happen next with Mrs. Buffington and Caesar.

"Let me try," I said.

"Don't frighten him. He's recovering from a nasty virus. His doctor said bland diet and keep him calm. Had to stop his fig squares; he's mad about fig squares. This is our first day out."

"Sorry." I took the dog treat from her and got down on my knees.

"Whatever you do, don't stick your head inside that door," Max said.

I knew he was right. I knew I should lead with an open palm holding Caesar's snack, but instead I stuck my head deep inside the dark compartment. I did it simply because it was the opposite of what Max had advised. As soon as I stretched my neck down and around so as to see where Caesar might be, the little mutt growled and leaped onto my scalp. His head and forelegs nestled into my hair while his miniature back legs dug into flesh. The right rear paw, like a pack of fish hooks, wedged itself into the top of my nose, pushing down on the bridge of my eyeglasses. The left back paw clung for dear life, grasping onto what little meat my forehead offered. Caesar's butt and tail were in a constant nervous twitter, pushing my eyeglasses toward the end of my nose. The pain from his talons was manageable, but the sudden attack triggered a scream out of me as I retreated, with Caesar clutching to my head for dear life.

"Oh my!" shrieked Mrs. Buffington.

"You're bleeding," Max said.

I stood and tasted drops of blood that had trickled down from my forehead. Then I felt an enormous release of pressure from my skull as Caesar leaped from my head onto Mrs. Buffington's shoulder. Given the size of Caesar's legs, the jump was simply incredible. The little guy must have put everything he had into it because he immediately lost control of his bowels. Still affected by the virus, out plopped three mustard-yellow dollops the size of quarters. One landed on my left foot, thankfully squarely atop my shoe. The second hit on the carpet, making an interesting highlight to the rust-colored flooring. The third bomb was far more problematic, landing precariously on the inside right lens of my eyeglasses, dripping a chunky river of dog diarrhea onto the side of my nose. With dog poop less than an inch from my eye, I slowly removed my glasses, and with my handkerchief wiped the fecal matter off my nose.

"I told you not to stick your head in there," Max said.

Afraid that Caesar would tear into Mrs. Buffington, I reached for the dog, who, sensing my approach, turned in my direction and saw not only me but Max, who was yelling that I should get checked for rabies and warning me about the terrible effects of dog crap entering open wounds. Caesar, making pained whimpers, scurried around Mrs. Buffington's neck and slipped down the back of her loose-fitting gray-blue polka-dot dress.

"Oh, dear," Mrs. Buffington screamed, and began gyrating in what could best be described as a spastic Macarena.

I flicked the dog poop off my glasses and cringed as it landed with a splash on a pair of suede, wool-lined, hundred-dollar gloves. "Let me help." I said, stepping toward her. She recoiled. I gently kicked the shit off my shoe. It landed close to the mess already on the carpet.

"No, you've done enough. Help! Help!" Mrs. Buffington waddled toward the front of the store, desperately trying to extract Caesar, who had squirmed down her backside and appeared to be getting comfortable at the small of her back.

I followed at a safe distance, trying to make eye contact with Van, who was ignoring all the action by pretending to re-hang suits.

"Leave her alone," Max shouted. "Go to the men's room and wash those cuts." Blood was seeping down both sides of my face, rolling with the curves so that droplets were falling on my upper lip and the carpet.

"Are you all right?" Lana asked a frenzied Mrs. Buffington, who approached her with fingers falling short of finding Caesar.

"Oh, this is awful. I never," Mrs. Buffington said.

"Let me help," Lana said, coming around the checkout counter and positioning herself between Mrs. Buffington and the front door. "Please."

"We got to get out of here," Max said. I stopped, realizing the worst thing right now would be for Caesar to see Max again. I made eye contact with Lana and hoped I communicated both my sorrow over the mess and my inability to help. She gave me a little nod, and I took a few steps back, keeping within earshot but hopefully out of view of both dog and mistress.

Lana managed to calm Mrs. Buffington and delicately released Caesar from his captivity. I could hear Mrs. Buffington thanking her and telling her that I must have transmitted some terribly upsetting vibes to her poor Caesar. "He's an extremely sensitive little dear. He knows when people don't like him or fear him. Rodney should see someone. I've never seen such a reaction. It's pathological, simply pathological. My goodness, I hope he's all right. I've never seen Caesar act like this. Truly pathological—dogs can sense fear."

"At least she's not thinking of suing the place," Max said.

I nodded, wiping blood from my face with my hand.

"At least not yet. You need to start listening to me," Max said, folding his arms across his chest.

I felt we were a safe distance from anyone's ears, so I said, "You seem like the last person I would ever take advice from."

"Look. I've always been the kind of guy who thought I was always right no matter what I was doing, even when I was screwing people, stealing, whatever. I always justified it. But I'm now here with you, and I just know that it's to help you."

Mrs. Buffington walked out of the store with Caesar safely tucked against her body. Before leaving, she gave Lana a hug and searched for me. Finally spotting me, a fresh handkerchief pressed to my forehead, she gave a big farewell wave. I could see little Caesar protesting as they left.

I went to the men's room to wash. Fortunately, the cuts had stopped bleeding before I started cleaning.

"Amazing, you are simply amazing," Max said.

"What?"

"I would have been swearing a blue streak. No little mutt would have got away with shitting in my face. I'd have drop-kicked that little hot dog out onto the street. He'd still be bouncing." I raised an eyebrow and pulled off my shoe, surprised at how little of Caesar's poop had remained. Unfortunately, where the leather creased, mustard-colored stains had dug in. "And I would have told Mrs. Buffington she needs to pay for me to see a doctor. Who knows what bacteria came squirting out that pooch's ass right into your face? You get any in your mouth? Because she looks like she's got a few bucks. Play it up big time." Max paused as I bunched up several paper towels and removed the last traces of Caesar's bowel movement from my loafer. Max continued, his voice softened. "I can't believe you didn't scare her into giving you a couple thousand. You know, blow things up, and she writes you a check to shut you up."

I looked over, making sure the door was closed. In a hushed voice, I said, "You literally scared the crap out of a little dog, and your concern is there's something wrong with me because I didn't try to scam the owner into giving me a few bucks."

"Hey, you don't know if the combination of his filthy paws and his infected shit doesn't turn you into some kind of one-in-a-million case of skin-eating whose-its. Then where will you be, Mr. High-and-Mighty?"

"With you." I laughed, and Max tried to look mad for a moment.

"Go ahead; make a joke. But if you get sick, remember who warned you."

"Max, don't you get tired of it?" I admired my clean shoe and slipped it back on.

"Of what?"

"Scamming."

"That, my dear boy, is what life is all about. Everyone is trying to pull something over on somebody, and some people try scamming everyone. And the sooner you realize it, the better off you'll be."

"You see, that's where you and I are fundamentally different."

"Please, kid, don't give me that happy horse shit about there's more to life than making money and taking care of number one." Suddenly Max rolled into a fetal position and clutched his ears. His body shook violently for several seconds. I readied myself for an attack by goblins, thinking some dark, cloaked, ghostly figures would come like a gust of wind crashing through the bathroom door, seize Max, and take him to hell. Then, just as suddenly as it began, it ended. Max stood with his eyes wide open and jaw hanging.

"The cat?"

"No, no. Much worse."

"What? Talk to me, Max."

Max shook his head as if clearing cobwebs and began in a whisper. "I've had it all wrong. This time, the voice—"

"The sexy voice?" I interrupted.

"No, the voice was my mother. She's been dead twenty years."

"Wow."

"It's more than wow, Rod. This is it for me. The voice was angry, saying I still didn't get it. I'm being given another chance to show that I'm not a total waste, and I don't get it. You see, when it first happened, the voice said, 'Listen, watch, help.' I took from that that I'm supposed to help you. I figured you were such a loser. No offense."

"None taken."

"See how hard you make it. You should be in my face, but you just let my insult pass, just like the hooker's drink screwing up your suit and that dog shitting in your face." Max shook his head.

"What do you mean, this is it?"

"I mean I need to show I understand what life's about. Me, a guy who knows he's got all the answers, has got to understand that I in fact don't know squat, and you, my son, are to teach me. And it was my mother speaking, a warning like all hell would be paid if I missed this chance. I feel scared but good. But really, really scared."

"Maybe they got it wrong," I protested.

"I don't think the guys on this side of life get it wrong."

"How am I supposed to help you? I'm just barely getting by with weekly therapy…" In midsentence, Max and I were joined by Van Paxton.

"Who are you talking to?"

"No one." I turned, opened the faucet, and began rinsing my hands.

"You said, 'with weekly therapy.'"

"I did?"

"Yeah, you did," Van said. His eyes avoided mine; he was a master of pointing out problems but never getting involved. He then proceeded to relieve himself.

Max put a finger to his lips and mouthed, 'Please,' as if I needed a reminder not to tell Van that I was talking to a ghost.

"I must have been thinking out loud. You know, with Mrs. Buffington's dog pooping in my face and cutting up my head. Need someone to talk to."

"Right. You also need to clean up that dog crap on the carpet before customers see it."

CHAPTER 7

CIAO, RODNEY

I left the men's room armed with enough paper towels to clean up after a Saint Bernard. The most difficult part of the cleanup was finding Caesar's droppings. Max proved helpful in narrowing the field of possible damage sites.

"Right here," Max said, raising a hand to halt my progress. He pointed to the two offending parties.

"Thanks," I whispered, and got down on my knees. I lifted 90 percent of the mess with my first swipe. What was left had merged on impact with the thick carpet fibers. The lion's share of Caesar's deposit I secured neatly in two sheets of paper towel and placed them under the lip of the glove display case, safely out of harm's way. I then proceeded with two more sheets to scrub the nasty remains out of the plush carpet. Max stood next to me, complaining that this was a job for a maintenance worker, not a hotshot salesman in $200 pants.

Incredibly, the more I rubbed, the larger the stain grew. It was as if Caesar had sowed poop seeds in the carpet and I was cultivating them.

"You're making it worse," Max said, as the spot expanded. "You need a strong detergent soap. Something is wrong—you're turning it from a speck into a blob."

I was about to unleash all of my frustrations on Max when Lana said, "Here." I looked up, and there she was with a bottle of some kind of Grime-Away in one hand and antiseptic wipes in the other. My eyes traveled from the curve of her knee up her thigh. I was suddenly hit by how wonderful it would be to have Lana always there for me.

"Here." She handed me the cleaner. A quick squirt, and presto, all signs of Caesar were gone. As I finished cleaning, Lana giggled about the crazy morning. She heaped embarrassing amounts of praise on me for keeping my cool after having a dog drop its load in my face.

"It was a small load," I said, which got both Lana and Max laughing.

"Let me look at you," she said. With me still on my knees, she bent down and examined the scratches. Her soft hands caressed my face. "Ah, this might sting a bit." She opened a two-inch square package and cleaned my forehead with a moist antiseptic wipe. "It'll kill any germs."

"Make your move, Rodney boy," Max said.

His timing was terrible. I was just about to make an inside joke about Van taking charge like any good manager would by running away. His words, which I'm sure were meant to be encouraging, hit me as criticism. Why was he coaching me? Did he think I needed his help? Was I so pathetic that after less than a day of knowing me, he summed me up as a loser with the ladies? What did he know about me? What did he know about Lana? What did he know about anything? My confidence shot, I just mumbled, "Thanks."

Rossini's *William Tell* Overture was now playing throughout the store, and just as the excitement of the chase was beginning to build, the music stopped, letting us know a customer had entered. Simon was still busy with his earlier customer, a portly, young executive who needed larger-size business suits.

Lana handed me two wipes. "I better get out front," she said, and I followed her beautiful body until she arrived at the checkout counter, where she greeted Mrs. Jags Carmello.

"Something that good isn't going to be around forever," Max said, admiring Lana.

Ramona Carmello, Jags's wife, a leggy, lean ex-model, looked perfect, as always. She was maybe forty-five, with a full bosom. Like a Hollywood starlet, she hid her identity behind designer sunglasses. Ramona always did something new with her hair. Today it was shoulder length, wavy, and honey colored, much softer than the reddish locks she had sported a few weeks ago. Behind her was Bruno, a bear of a man who was always by her side. Bruno, I assumed, functioned as one of Jags's bodyguards. In all the years he had accompanied members of the Carmello family here, I had never seen his expression change; it was always one of dead earnestness. There he was, a neckless hulk with hands larger than my head. Simon, an admirer of the local mob, had shared with me that years ago Bruno did time for manslaughter. He had let loose one punch to the side of this guy's head and end of story. Simon was jealous that Jags and his wife always asked for me to wait on them.

Also at the door, with his eyes on Lana, was Slick, the Carmellos' driver. According to Simon, Slick had earned his name by his legendary escapes from law enforcement. Once he had eluded police by navigating a hot Impala up and down city streets and sidewalks without injuring any pedestrians or damaging any property. He always dressed in black, with sunglasses resting on the top of his curly, raven-colored head. A thumb-width gold chain hung from his neck. Everything about Slick said, "I'm cool." I imagined Bruno had an intense dislike for his flashy colleague and wondered what conversations between these two apparent opposites were like during their downtime waiting for Jags or Ramona.

"Mrs. Carmello." I smiled, and she removed her sunglasses, showing the most beautiful green eyes. My smile started to become awkwardly long as my gaze strayed beyond Mrs. Carmello, fixing instead on the late morning light, which added a sparkle to Lana's hair. Ramona winked, causing my stomach to knot. The last thing I wanted was a wink from the wife of the man who ran the largest local organized crime family, a man whom the DA was forever bringing charges against, a man who after each arraignment proudly announced to reporters, "These bums got nothing." He was someone who on more than one occasion, after helping him select a suit, I found myself fantasizing about hiring him to kill my mother.

"Rodney, so glad you're working today." She gave me a hug. I noticed Slick undressing Lana with his eyes as she beamed innocent hospitality. "What happened to your forehead?"

"Oh, it's nothing. A little dog got excited, and well, it's a long story."

"Those cuts look tender. You want some aloe? I always have aloe," she said, clutching her handbag.

"No, no, I'm fine."

Ramona gave a look of doubt, and I again reassured her that there was no need for concern.

Max stood between Ramona and Bruno, making goo-goo eyes and pretending to grab her ass. I thought, If Jags knew, he'd kill him again.

Ramona gushed like an excited child, her words spilling out, "You'll never believe what's happening."

Before I could say anything, she blurted, "Finally Jags agreed to go someplace besides Vegas. Italy, three weeks! I can't believe it. It's a dream. We almost went five years ago, but he was worried about some Dominicans or Colombians, or somebody muscling in on his north county action, so instead of two weeks in Italy, we spent four days in Vegas. He lost twenty g's and bellyached the whole time flying back about the blackjack table. Everybody in first class was gawking at us, with Jags crying about his getting screwed at the table. I tells him to hush up, and he squeezes my face like he's trying to see if he can pop my fucking brains out. He lets go, and I tells him, 'No more Vegas.' That was the first and last time he ever pulled that shit with me. I didn't speak to him until we got home. Then the first thing I did, Bruno is unloading suitcases, Jags lights a cigar, and then I stick the Glock he keeps in the dining room, under the good silver, in his face and scream so they can hear me back in Vegas, 'You ever get rough with me, and I'll fucking kill you.' I thought he was going to shit himself. Well, anyway that was five years ago, and this is now. Hello, Roma! I thought I'd never get him to go. Italy, three weeks—I can't believe it."

"Sounds wonderful."

"We're going everywhere. I thought he could use some new casual clothes, you know. Everything he's got is for business. He's all gray or navy-blue suits, white shirts—boring. He could go to a month of funerals and not wear the same suit twice."

"Sure, his lightweight summer suits should be okay for the Mediterranean. Maybe a couple of sweaters just in case the evenings are cool," I said, guiding her toward knit shirts and casual pants.

As we took our first steps away from Lana, I could hear Slick start in a syrupy voice, "So you'd never guess what happened to me this morning."

"What?"

"No, guess..."

Their voices were lost to the background music and distance. Bruno and Max trailed behind us. Max was seriously taken by Ramona, licking his lips, looking as if he were about to jump her.

Ramona slipped her sunglasses into her purse and searched for any nearby ears before speaking. She gave me another wink and motioned me to come closer. "Jags is so relieved. You know that son of a bitch DA makes it personal the way he goes after Jags. Even the newspapers, they make Jags seem like he was Charlie Manson, but even they say the DA had a score to settle. It's like Jags can't even spit on the sidewalk. This time that bastard had everything going his way. The judge, an old fart, I thought was going to croak when the verdict came in. Everyone had my Jags counted out. The guys," she said, casting an eye back toward Slick, who was gesturing with his arms to a laughing Lana, "figured he was going away for years. At least twenty, right, Bruno?" Bruno's boulder of a head gave a slight nod. "Everyone is thinking it's over, so Jags..." Ramona paused and practically put her face on my shoulder. "You can never repeat this, but Jags was scared. You say a word and…"

"Don't worry." I noticed Lana had her back to Slick, who appeared to be putting a necklace on her.

Ramona straightened up. "Thank God for Bruno." She smiled his way and stopping at a display of golf shirts, looked me in the eye and said, "You don't know the half of it. You know the work he's in; the competition's all sharks. They see a guy scared, it's like blood in the water. Even guys you trust, you can't trust them anymore if they think you're scared. Eat you alive. What do they say, Bruno, you swim with the sharks, and sooner or later the sharks…what do they say, Bruno?"

Bruno shrugged and said, "Sharks have you for dinner."

"Hey, Rod," Max said, and turned his head toward Slick and Lana. "You see what that little son of a bitch is doing?"

"Terrible," I said to Ramona, giving Max a look as if to say, "What do you want from me?"

"So he promised if he got out of this mess, he'd take me anywhere I wanted. 'You name it baby, and it's yours,' he said."

"Sounds great."

"Bruno, what do you think?" Ramona asked, holding up a canary-yellow golf shirt.

"It don't seem like the boss."

"Right, maybe the navy and the white," Ramona said. Bruno nodded and I fished out some choices for her.

"Maybe four or five; nothing flashy." Ramona looked at my selections and said, "Good. Now some pants. I'm so excited we're going to Rome, Florence, Venice, Capri…"

"In Capri, you have to go to the Blue Grotto."

"Really?"

"It's out of this world. And the flowers in Capri, the sunsets." I shook my head in awe.

"You've been?"

"This guy is scoring like you read about," Max hissed, motioning with his head toward Slick and Lana.

"No, I wish. I just love watching those PBS travel shows. It's like being there." I smiled and nodded. "And Venice, what a city, all those beautiful buildings right in the water." I then went into a ten-minute discourse about St. Marks, the Bridge of Sighs, and then Florence, the Uffizi Museum, the Ponte Vecchio, and then Rome, the Sistine Chapel, the Pieta, the square at St. Peter's, the fountains, and on and on. "You are so lucky."

"Hmm. Jags is thinking three weeks, and he doesn't have to worry about getting whacked. Only reason he's going is because he promised me. He's concerned about the business here, I understand, but even the president takes a vacation. He's so crazy he asked the travel agent if the hotels served bacon and eggs for breakfast. I said, 'Is that all you're worried about?' He said, 'I've been out of the can nineteen years, and every day I have bacon and eggs for breakfast. It's working.' Ugh."

"Once he's there, I'm sure he'll get into it. You know, when in Rome."

Ramona smirked and said, "This'll sound crazy, but the way you're talking, I wish you were coming with us." Then she winked.

"Look out, Romeo," Max muttered.

"You could be our personal guide. Imagine, Jags, Bruno, you, and me. The guys could sit around drinking grappa, and you and me could explore Italy."

"It would be fun, but…"

"But what? Jags knows you know who he is, so he'd trust us. He thinks guys like you are either, eh—I mean, would have made a good priest. He said that the last time you helped him with that suit he wore when his lawyer gave his closing. Jags said, 'That kid Rodney, he's got a face you can trust should've been a priest.' All I got to do is say, 'Jags, that kid Rodney knows all about Italy. He could show us the real Italy.' I know what Jags would think; it's great. I'll be safe in those boring museums with Rodney, and he could have some fun with Bruno."

"You're too kind, but I'm, I'm not really able to travel."

"A free trip." Ramona wrapped her arm around my elbow. "It'll be fun." She entwined the fingers of her left hand around the fingers of my right hand and started singing. Her right arm released my elbow and hugged my waist. For a few seconds, we were dancing to her giggling version of "That's Amore." I, with eyes begging forgiveness and understanding, looked over to Bruno, who pretended to be concerned about how he was holding

Jags's new shirts. The thought of Bruno's hands around my neck stopped my feet.

"Be careful, Rod; this babe is in a different league," Max said.

Ramona continued dancing, trying to drag me along. She stopped, began laughing, clutched my arm, and laughed out, "We'd have a blast."

"I can't really leave my mother; she's not well."

"Oh, shit—because I like you, Rodney. I really like you. You must think I'm crazy, but I feel comfortable around you. You're not like the guys I'm used to." Ramona's eyes slowly traveled from my waist to my face. She smiled, and for a few seconds, her green eyes stared into mine. It hit me how empty my life was, and then a fear seized me that I might soon be losing that empty life. I imagined Bruno telling Jags that I had made a play for his wife. Then right before they board their flight for Rome, Bruno stops by, snaps my neck, and dumps me in a swamp.

"My mother doesn't have long to live." I felt my heart pushing through my throat. My legs shook the way spent muscles do when forced beyond their capacities. I prayed Bruno would take pity on me, a nobody salesman caring for his dying mother.

"So sorry," she said, and patted my cheek. "What do you think, Bruno?" She turned and held up a pair of white knee-length shorts.

"I can't see the boss in them."

"But you know a lot about Italy?" Ramona asked me, and pulled out a pair of long-legged beige Giorgio Armani's.

"That's better," Bruno said, referring to the wardrobe selections.

"Not really," I protested. "I enjoy watching the travelogues. Last month they featured Italy, from the Alps to Sicily."

"You see, that's what Jags needs." Ramona wiggled over toward me, looking at the rack of trousers. "He needs some culture, needs to broaden his interests."

I collected all the items Ramona had selected and escaped for the checkout. I kept telling myself that nothing had happened. My legs felt steadier. I could hear Slick and was glad that they would soon be leaving. I couldn't excuse myself and let Lana handle the sale from here. No, with Ramona Carmello, I had to be there at her side until she and the hit squad were out the door. If I left, I'd be a nervous wreck until I saw her or Jags again, wondering if I had offended her. But if I stayed, there would be the possibility of a parting embrace, another wink, or more invitations to sunny Italy.

Slick smiled at our approach and continued speaking to Lana, "The best Alfredo sauce in this one-horse town is over at Michael's. I know the guy isn't even Italian, but it's the best. But if you want out-of-this-world seafood, it's the Verona. Maybe you'd like to go sometime?"

"See, that's how it's done," Max whispered in my ear.

"Oh, let me think about it," Lana said, and blushed.

"No hurry, they've been in business seventy-five years." Slick laughed the way cocky men who always have something to say do.

Slick's banter hit me hard. The blood was pounding at my temples when my phone vibrated. I pulled it out of my pocket and checked the number. It was home. The only calls I ever received at work were from home and usually from Elizabeth, telling me she had called an ambulance because Mother was knocking on heaven's door.

"So sorry, I have to take this," I said, and stepped away from the counter. Ramona lowered an eyebrow, winked, and gave a sweet goodbye. I prayed that Bruno and Slick had missed it, but both of them looked my way and made sure our eyes met. Slick's look was more of disbelief, while Bruno's seemed to be saying in his quiet, threatening way, I can hurt you so bad that you'd wish you were dead. A cold sweat started rolling down my spine.

"She wants you, Romeo," Max said, giving a fiendish chuckle.

I bowed and continued my retreat, anticipating, with a degree of unexpected joy, Elizabeth telling me, 'Oh, Mr. Rodney, I have bad news.' That feeling was immediately replaced by thoughts of what a rotten bastard I was, hoping for the worst. Before I could answer the call, Ramona cackled, "Think about Italy, ooh la la." She stretched out an elegant arm as if saying goodbye while trying to lure me to her.

Bruno's left eyebrow rose a quarter of an inch, and I knew he thought something more than quality men's clothing was being offered to his boss's wife.

I gave a nervous smile and backed away, whispering "Hello" into the phone.

"Oh, Mr. Rodney, I'm sorry to bother you." It was an excited Elizabeth. "If you are busy, call me when you have a moment, but we have, I'm afraid, trouble here— big trouble. I am so sorry."

I gave Ramona, who was watching me, a little wave and turned to one side. I needed to avoid acting in any way that she might construe as rude, yet I needed to communicate to Slick and Bruno my complete indifference. To Elizabeth I said, "No, what is it?"

"Your mother is a nervous wreck, Mr. Rodney—all day a wreck."

"Slow down, Elizabeth."

"She believes you have gone mad. I'm in the bathroom. She did not want me to call. I told her my stomach is upset, and that's no lie, Mr. Rodney. Your mother is not going to drive me mad. But all day she asks, 'Can you stay the night?'"

"So sorry."

"Yes, do not worry, I have battled worse."

"What is she saying?"

"She believes you will pretend to be mad and then kill her in her sleep. Temporary insanity, she said, over and over. She is petrified. I can't get her to calm down.

I asked her what is your proof, and she described, forgive me, Mr. Rodney, some very strange happenings, very strange. I do not believe it. I know you are a good man. She is so certain you acted like a man, how can I say this?....possessed."

"It's nothing like that, I thought I saw my father. It was a mistake. That's all."

"She wants me to stay over. Keep an eye on you."

"Can you?"

"I will have to talk to my James. You know James; he expects his supper every night. Tonight he will be coming over to have midnight chicken with you and Miss Audrey. What shall I do?"

"Nothing."

"Nothing?"

"Elizabeth, in a few days, Mother will see I mean her no harm, and she will be back to her old...self." I had to catch myself from saying *miserable.*

Elizabeth said confidently, "But tonight, I will tell her I'm letting you know what she believes. If the robber knows the people know he's a robber, then he must leave or change his ways. The robber never strikes when eyes are upon him."

"Are you okay?"

"Yes, yes, I told her you are a good man."

"Thank you."

Before I put my phone away, Max said, "What's up? You look like hell."

I motioned to Max that I was going to the men's room. I waved to Van, who was coming out of Mr. Waite's office, alerting him to my need to take care of business.

"So how about that? Italy with that babe," Max said as we entered the empty restroom.

"That babe is Jags Carmello's wife. Jags, local mob boss."

"You play Italy right with them, and maybe they could set you up in your own place. Imagine, Rodney's Fine Men's Store. I like it."

"Do you really think I'm the kind of guy who can play with mobsters? You know, Max, people who kill people, steal, sell drugs. You've seen me in action: giving out Halloween candies, brushing up on Civil War History, getting horny over hookers male and female, chasing loose-bowelled dachshunds. So of course you can see me touring Italy with a couple of killers and the frustrated wife of a crime boss."

"You need to take some chances."

"Were you nuts before you died?"

"Depends who you ask."

"Well, I'm not going to Italy as Ramona Carmello's traveling companion."

Max shook his head disapprovingly.

"You can think being pals with Jags is a great idea, but you have the luxury of already being dead."

"Huh?"

"Listen, the little I know about Jags is that you don't want to give him problems because he buries his problems, and there's no way I want him to know me well enough to be a problem for him."

CHAPTER 8

SPIKE ON THE WARPATH

I headed to the back of the store near the dressing rooms and positioned myself next to a mannequin wearing a full-length, chestnut-colored leather coat. No one but Max could see me there. I hoped to get a few minutes of quiet reflection about the home front and to attempt to determine if I had anything to fear from Jags Carmello. My mind skidded from one improbable event to the next. Since Max's arrival my humdrum life had become a cauldron of chaos. Images of an outraged Mrs. Buffington and her frightened Caesar collided with thoughts of Max, and then there was last night with Mother. These were then pushed aside by Ramona Carmello seducing me, only to have us face Jags. Then there was Max. Then there was lusting for Beatrice and Dinky. In the midst of this kaleidoscope, the idea that Mother was hallucinating began to germinate as a possible response to her accusations.

Just as Max cleared his throat to get my attention, an exaggeratedly lusty voice pierced my skull from the front of the store. "Is Rodney here? Please, girl, this is lock-the-doors-and-shut-off-the-lights important. You listening, blondie? Because if Rodney's here, he needs to find himself a hole and go hide."

"Beatrice?" I mumbled to myself. Her presence here confirmed that my world had collapsed. Close to tears, my legs buckled under what appeared to be a new boat-load of trouble.

"Oh yeah," Max said, betraying a twinge of alarm that made me realize he was actually concerned about me.

My ears blocked out Mozart's Clarinet Concerto, which softly played on the store's public address system. It was as if Beatrice and Lana's voices were hardwired to my brain. I heard Lana's voice tremble as she gave a hesitant "Yes."

I imagined Beatrice tapping her two-inch long gold nails on the counter as she said, "I need to see him—need to see him pronto. This is an emergency, blondie. You get it?"

"To the men's room," Max ordered, like a combat veteran after spotting the enemy.

I took a deep breath and proceeded to do the opposite of what Max had advised, taking a step to the front of the store.

"Don't be crazy. That broad is trouble, more trouble than you can handle. If I was living, I wouldn't be caught dead with her."

I threw Max a skeptical look.

"Disease," he snapped.

It was as if Max's rejection of Beatrice reinforced my gut reaction to see what she wanted despite my shaking knees. I took a few more baby steps forward. Max, flailing cape and arms, waved me back. I made my way to the store's center aisle, where I saw Beatrice and shuddered. Beatrice held what looked like a cloth against her left cheek. She towered over Lana, who wore a nervous smile and shifted her weight from foot to foot behind the main horseshoe-shaped front checkout counter. Simon gave me a raised eyebrow and smirked as I walked by him. At that moment, Lana saw me and pointed in my direction. Beatrice lowered the cloth from her face; although I was still a good ten feet from her, I could see her face was distorted. As I grew closer, an enormous welt appeared where her jaw and ear met.

Beatrice filled the store with a mighty roar. "Rodney, you've got to get your ass out of here!" Her voice echoed in my head. I wanted to take her by the hand and run away.

"Call the police," Max implored.

Lana took two steps back and pressed her behind against the opposite counter. She and Beatrice both encouraged me forward. Lana's crystal-blue eyes filled with terror. Beatrice swiped her arm dramatically in my direction. I knew Max was right: Beatrice was out of my league. My being with her was like being recruited to perform heart surgery while visiting an ill relative in the hospital. This long, lean lady of the night made a grimace and said, "Spike is at war with you."

"Yikes," I said.

"Yeah, yikes," Beatrice repeated frowning.

"Your face, what happened?"

"Spike wants to kill you."

"Kill me?"

"He believes there's something going on between us. Believes I got some unprofessional ideas vis-à-vis you and me."

"Get a gun," Max barked.

"'Vis-à-vis'?" I asked, staring at the monster bruise on the side of her face.

"'In relation to'—it's French, baby," Beatrice said.

I shrugged and said, "Warpath?"

"Spike is bipolar. You ask me, both poles are plenty loopy. He hasn't been taking his meds. He was getting them free at the clinic over on Hopkins, but when they found out he was working the waiting room, they banned him. There's a scary security guard named Felix, big crazy Puerto Rican who says he sees Spike, he'll hold him for the cops. Felix would love to have a go at Spike. They're worse than fire and water. Spike says he's going to kill that fat son of a bitch. Never seen Spike spinning out of control like this. Before I met you, he tried to set me up with some whack job who had a German shepherd. I told him I only dance with two-legged dogs.

Since we parted ways this morning, he's got you on the brain. Wanted to..."

I raised a hand and hollered, "Wait!"

"Tell her to call someone who cares," Max said, his arms crossed and jaw clenched.

I looked at Lana, who was inching her way toward the counter's opening. I assumed she was preparing a speedy exit strategy.

"Let's go outside," I said.

"That's it; tell the queen of the boulevard of broken dreams to hit the road," Max said, nodding his head determinedly.

"It may not be safe," Beatrice said, her eyes darting from side to side.

"This is a business. You can't stay here," I said, and bit my lower lip.

"Stay public! Witnesses," Max screamed.

I was more concerned about a scene in the store with Beatrice. I was not appreciating her fear of Spike. I, in my smug little world, had nothing to relate to her and Spike. I repeated, "Let's talk outside."

"If Spike comes, we split in opposite directions. Run, hide, and call the police." Beatrice dabbed at her injury with the damp handkerchief and winced. "He doesn't realize his strength. He hears you calling nine-one-one, he'll turn and run, crazy or not."

"You know it's bad when streetwalkers tell you to call the cops," Max said, his nose wrinkling under his mask.

Lana held a hand in front of her mouth as if holding back a scream. Her body was poised at an angle, one foot out from behind the counter, ready to run as fast as she could to the furthest reaches of the store. She shook her head no, as if completely overwhelmed by what she was hearing.

Van and Simon stood at a safe distance, with arms folded across their chests.

"I'll just be a minute," I said to no one in particular.

"Don't be crazy," Max said, standing in front of me as if to prevent my leaving.

I pointed to the entrance. "We'll be okay out there the street is so busy."

Beatrice shook her head no but moved toward the front entrance. "I can't live like this," Beatrice said, throwing up her hands.

I followed her outside, staying one step back. Once outside, Beatrice looked over her shoulder as if asking where to go. I wanted to be out of view of Van and Simon, so we walked a few feet away from the storefront.

"He's going to come here," Beatrice said.

"Why?"

"He's in a manic cycle. Nothing makes sense. He thinks because I didn't come on strong to you and you were kind to me that we got something going on."

"I thought you did come on strong," I said, surprised that the sound of her voice was so pleasing to me.

"No, I was real friendly, not pay-me friendly. Sort of come si come sa. Spike says you had a screwy look, like you were looking to get it on with me, and then I act like Miss Congeniality. He thinks maybe I'm taking some action on the side. Wouldn't be the first girl to try to keep something for herself. If he only knew, I've been skimming for the last year, saving to relocate. Send something every now and then to my sister, Patrice, down in Baltimore. She's raising three kids on a shoestring." Beatrice looked at me as if to say this too will pass. "But with you, it's all in his head. I'm not conning you, Rodney."

I fought back an urge to hug her and meekly said, "I know."

"Conning—hold onto your wallet. Here comes the money pitch from Empress Easy-Peasy; whatever you do, give her nothing," Max hollered, and began to snigger. The next thing, Max was crouched between Beatrice's legs. His nose and mouth were right at her knees, just below her hem line.

"Thanks," Beatrice said, and tapped my arm, sending warm fuzzy sensations through me.

Max slowly rose from under Beatrice's miniskirt, and said, "Sorry, I will listen and shut up. Yes, she's one of God's children. I know, I know, we all have a lot to work on. Nobody's perfect. Promise, I'll try harder."

"But unless Spike runs into other trouble, he'll come looking for you and me. There's no telling what he'll do. He nearly killed Dinky. Gave that little darling such a beating—found two bills on him. Wham!"

"Bills?" I asked.

"Ben Franklins."

"Maybe he'll calm down."

"No, he says if this little fancy-pants means nothing, let's go rip him off at his fancy-ass Haynesworth and Waite's. Says it full of spite, full of rage. Says for me to keep you busy while he walks off with a few suits. I tell him he's crazy. Cameras all over the place, and we's both known to the cops. That's when he punched me. Never saw it coming. I think my jaw is broke. Hurts like a mother. Can't live like this."

"Why did you come here?"

"To warn you." Beatrice paused, looked away, and said, "I don't know, I thought maybe you could help me."

Max violently shook his head no and frantically flapped his arms.

"Help?"

"Bus ticket to Baltimore. I just sent Patrice my last hundred dollars a few days ago. I'm flat busted. I'll pay you back. I know you must think I'm crazy to ask you. But you got the sweetest eyes. Like they're saying, 'Please let me help.'" Before I could say anything, a look of horror seized Beatrice, and she yelled, "Shit!"

Charging toward us as if attack dogs were at his heels was Spike. He was wearing a maroon suit with wide lapels and a silk mint-green shirt. He held a handgun that reminded me of an Old West six-shooter. I imagined my face being blown off and feared I would wet myself. My feet began rattling in my shoes, and my tongue shriveled, preventing speech. I looked over at Beatrice, who, upon seeing Spike, sprawled across the pavement at my feet. Her head was turned away from the approaching maniac, and her legs bent at the knee, making her seem completely vulnerable. One of her six-inch heels had come off and was a foot away from her. I fought the urge to join her on the pavement. As Spike neared, his eyes grew larger and more intense. I was facing an armed lunatic.

"You poisoning my well, motherfucker? Nobody poisons Spike Drake's well. No fucking way." Spike raised his revolver.

The gun loomed large in my face. I closed my eyes and prepared to die, waiting for the highlights of my life to flash before me. They did not. I pressed my eyelids tighter, heard the chatter of my teeth and the blood pounding in my head.

Max screamed, "Call the police."

Later Max told me how I survived. About three feet away from me, as Spike took aim and fired, he closed his eyes, took a step forward, and tripped over Beatrice's shoe. His stumble raised his hand enough for the bullet to sail, ever so slightly, over my head, hitting a streetlight twenty yards south. My mind at the time of Spike's assault was the consistency of a bag of wet yarn. My thoughts focused for a moment on my grandfather, and my heart smiled. My frightened, rubbery legs were unable to support me. The shot's sound, like a clap of thunder, rang in my ears. I fainted. Max informed me later that Spike, seeing me on the ground, must have figured I was history and thankfully did not bother to check for blood or signs of life. He just screamed, "Fancy-pants bastard," turned, and ran across the street. He kept running, Max told me, eventually dissolving into the urban horizon.

"Pleeeease don't die," I heard an emotionally spent Beatrice moan. Then I felt large soft palms lifting my head off the pavement. I opened my eyes slowly, still scared that Spike might be close at hand. Beatrice caressed my head, which was nestled in her lap. "Thank God—you're alive," she hollered, and in that moment, I was very grateful to be alive.

Max leaned over me. I could hear fear in his usually glib voice, "Crazy madman—Rodney, you've got to call nine-one-one."

Beatrice and I rose together. The missing shoe caused her to stand lopsided. We hung onto each other. I searched for Spike. "He's gone," Beatrice said, holding me steady while she stretched her leg out and hooked her toes around the strap of the wayward high heel that had saved my life. Incredibly agile, I thought as she flipped the shoe toward her, catching it in her free hand in a graceful motion and slipping her foot into it.

"Are you okay?" I asked.

Beatrice started crying, and her head plopped onto my shoulder. I wrapped my arms around her and gently patted her back. Through tears, she confessed her certainty that we both would be killed. She wailed uncontrollably for a minute about how this life would eventually do her in. I massaged her back and told her it would be all right.

Max, vying for my attention with arms waving, repeatedly yelled in his loudest dead man's voice, "Nine-one-one—call the *police*."

"He will kill me," Beatrice said, and her body trembled as if a Canadian cold front had blasted her.

I stepped away from her, inhaled a delicious lavender perfume, and thought, How much could a bus ticket to Baltimore possibly cost?

Max, as if reading my mind, made a time-out signal with his hands and shoved them in my face.

"If he kills me. If you see in the papers 'City Prostitute Killed,' keep reading. Or if you see Beatrice Ridge has been killed. That's my name. Call the police, promise."

I nodded. Overwhelmed with pity and love, I wrapped my arms around Beatrice. And just as I was about to kiss her, Lana's angelic voice whispered from the front door, pulling me back both physically and emotionally. "Rodney, Mr. Waite wants to see you." Then, full of fear, she asked, "Should I call the police?"

I looked at Beatrice, and she gave her head a little shake, no.

"No, just a misunderstanding," I mumbled, and looked to Beatrice for confirmation.

Beatrice nodded, and I released her.

I then turned toward Lana. I could tell she didn't want our eyes to meet. It was as if she had caught me in an embarrassing moment and wanted to lessen my misery. "You don't want the police?" she asked, sounding alarmed.

"No, it's a family matter."

"Family matter?"

"You know families; it'll pass."

Lana shook her head in disbelief and mumbled, "Those two are family?"

I nodded and said, "Different fathers." I then turned To Beatrice and said, "Baltimore."

"It's my only chance," Beatrice said.

"I want to help."

"It's ninety-three dollars."

"I haven't that much on me."

"Rodney," Lana said. Our eyes met, and she lowered her eyebrows in a way that reminded me that the boss wasn't a patient man.

I raised my index finger, asking her to wait, and said to Beatrice, "I live at Twenty-Three Dakota, first floor. You can wait there for me."

"Are you crazy!" Max screamed. He tried to grab my shoulders, but being a spirit, he could only gesture and curse.

Beatrice's mouth dropped, and she tried to speak.

I put a finger to my lips to silence her and said, "My mother and her caretaker, Elizabeth, are there. I'll call and tell them you're coming. It'll be safe there."

"Why don't you just hand her your bank book?" Max asked, his hands clasped as if he were about to start praying.

"Rodney, Mr. Waite," Lana insisted, and motioned with her head to the store.

"Yes, tell Mr. Waite I'll be just a minute."

Lana shook her head and went back to the store.

"Big mistake," Max moaned.

"I can't," Beatrice said, and took a step back.

"You said he'll kill you."

Beatrice nodded and her eyes filled with tears.

"He almost killed me," I said.

"I shouldn't have come here," Beatrice said, and wiped a tear from her cheek.

"The first thing I've heard that wasn't totally nuts," Max said, and nodded as if he recognized progress. Then he dropped to his knees and hid his face in his hands. His shoulders heaved as if he were bawling.

"Beatrice, I don't think it was an accident I ran into you this morning. I think I'm supposed to help you."

Beatrice dropped to the ground next to Max and hugged my legs. A torrent of tears came out as she clung to me like a drowning sailor catching hold of a piece of driftwood. I gently patted her head and took out my cell phone. "It'll all work out. You'll see," I said.

Max stood up and looked confused and frightened.

I smiled at him and for the first time, maybe in my entire life, felt truly alive. I took hold of Beatrice's upper arm and helped her to her feet.

Max whispered in a sympathetic tone, "My mother said what you're doing is beautiful and for me to shut up and learn." He shrugged and crossed his arms.

"For me? You'll do this for me?" Beatrice asked in a soft, childlike voice.

I nodded and smiled as my phone rang. It was Elizabeth. "How's Mother?"

"She's sitting with me, watching our soaps. Every once in a while, she'll ask if I'm staying the night. I tell her we will all feast on my midnight chicken and see what my James thinks. She says she doesn't trust you. It's very sad, Mr. Rodney, very sad."

"Tell her I love her, would never harm her."

"I know."

"Tell her right now."

Elizabeth hollered, "It's Rodney; he says he loves you. Says he would never harm you." There was a pause. I could hear Mother's voice but could not make out what she was saying. Elizabeth came back and said, "She's more like her old self."

"What did she say?"

"I can't repeat it, but she's better."

"What did she say?"

"I can't repeat it, but believe me, she's better."

"Good. Tell her I know she's afraid, but she doesn't have to be afraid of me or anything."

"I don't think that's such a good idea, Mr. Rodney."

"Please, Elizabeth, tell her."

"She's right here."

Mother got on the phone and sounded stronger than usual. "Rodney, you come to your senses? You ready to tell the truth about last night? Because I'm ready to have you committed to the loony bin."

"I love you, and I'll explain everything tonight. But for now, don't be frightened of anything. I've had the strangest day of my life."

"You taking drugs?"

"No."

"You sure?"

"Of course I'm sure. But I need to help someone and she's...a little different."

"You in trouble?"

"No, but she is. Her name is Beatrice, and she's going to wait at our apartment until I get home from work."

"What kind of trouble?"

"I'll explain when I get home."

"How do you know this Beatrice?"

"She was desperate, and I offered to help her."

"What do we look like, the Red Cross?"

"I know I have to do this."

"A stranger?"

"She's desperate."

"What's her problem?"

I paused and thought, Maybe I should have just told Elizabeth.

"The longer you hem and haw, the worse this Beatrice sounds," Mother said, and I could hear in her voice the old joy she received from another's misfortune.

"A friend of hers is kind of violent and may try to hurt her."

"Is she a looker?"

"Yes, but…"

"It's about time you brought someone home. You should have said something before about a girlfriend. I was thinking your balls had dried up and fallen off, like overripe plums."

"It's not like that with Beatrice."

"Of course it's not; it can never be like that. No, why make an old lady happy?"

"Don't get mad or scared."

"Oh shit, Rodney—now you're making me scared."

"She's black."

"Oh, hell, if she's a looker, and you like her, I don't care if she's purple."

"I'm just helping her, Mom. It's not what you think."

"Okay, I'm missing my show. Need to see if the good-looking doctor who almost died last week gets dumped by the cute brunette who's really his niece who he never knew. But I still want answers about last night."

CHAPTER 9

CAESAR CATCHES A RIDE

"I saw from the window," Lana said, as I entered the store. Her voice was hushed and choked, which I found reassuring and sexy. I looked furtively, not sure what she saw and too afraid to ask. "When he stuck that gun in your face, I thought I was going to die with you. It was so horrible. My knees are still shaking."

"Oh," I said, wondering if there was a woman on this planet who could love a man who faints in the face of danger.

"I couldn't bear to watch. I closed my eyes and then heard it. It sounded like a bomb. I started crying and still am, inside. I imagined your face blown off like you see in those awful movies teenage boys love. Finally, when I found the courage to look, there you were on the sidewalk with that—that—whatever she is comforting you." Lana shuddered.

"Ta-da, I'm still here," I said, and made a triumphant flourish with my hands. I immediately felt uncomfortably stupid with my stab at humor.

"Who was that?" Lana asked, sounding much calmer.

"Play this right, Rodney, my boy, for I see your sexual drought coming to a beautiful end," Max said.

"The shooter?"

"Did you know the shooter?" A look of disbelief came over Lana's face.

"It was all a terrible misunderstanding," I said in my most understated manner.

"Oh," Lana said, her eyes demanding more information.

"Tell her he's wanted in nine states. That you've uncovered a major drug operation and are working with the FBI, state and local law enforcement. Tell her the cops will soon be picking up Spike, and it's all because of you, one brave, unselfish John Q. Citizen. Go ahead they love it, and there's nobody to..." In midsentence Max stopped talking and began making defensive gestures as if trying to protect his head from slaps.

I searched for a way of having it make sense and putting Lana's mind at peace. "It's a long story. He needs his meds and got me mixed up with someone else, and one thing led to another." I smiled and gave a meek, uninformed shrug. Max was still trying to defend himself, the way a child might from an angry mother.

"And the woman? She looks like a..."

"That's Beatrice; she works for the shooter, and he thought Beatrice was interested in me." Lana had a confused glazed look. "It's all just a big, crazy misunderstanding."

"Okay, okay, sorry," Max said, on his knees. "I understand—watch and learn."

"Why would he think that?" Lana's head jolted back as if the thought of me and Beatrice together repulsed her.

"It was an innocent misunderstanding."

"She's a hooker?" Lana whispered, as if scared by the possibilities of where this might take her.

"She's trying to leave that life."

"So you two are friends?" Lana wrinkled her nose.

"More like survivors of a disaster. Yes, I'd say we have the bond of a mutual disaster."

"I know it's your business, but how could you get mixed up with those two?"

"Where to begin?" I gave a pained looked.

"You don't have to," she said, her words washed over me with disappointment.

"No, it was purely a case of being in the wrong place at the wrong time. We bumped into each other, literally, and I spilled her drink and bought her a new one. Her pimp, the shooter, has serious mental problems and thought that we had something going on based on the way she was looking at me. But there was nothing; it was just an accident, and I wanted to do the right thing." As I explained, I felt as if I were betraying Beatrice. "She came here to warn me. She's trying to leave all this. Has a sister in Baltimore, hopes to make a fresh start."

"She told you all this as you were buying her a coffee."

I said sheepishly, "Her pimp, Spike, wanted to kill us both. That has a way of pulling people together."

"Spike?"

I nodded.

Lana sighed. "He could have killed you." Her eyes filled.

"I'm okay."

"How? The gun was right in your face. I screamed. Simon went to get Van, and both of them stood by the phone."

"By the phone?"

"I guess to call the police. But then the guy missed. They didn't want the bad publicity," Lana said, as if now only truly realizing that I was all right.

"Dumb luck."

"Miracles—I started praying as soon as that nut arrived," Lana's voice cracked as she shook her head and blessed herself.

"Me too," Max said.

"That makes three of us," I said, and chuckled.

"Three of us?"

"Beatrice, I'm sure, must have been praying with us."

"Oh, well. Mr. Waite still needs to see you," Lana said. For the first time in my life, someone besides my grandfather was looking at me like I was special.

"Ask her out," Max insisted, and then nervously looked around as if getting ready for an attack.

"Maybe after work we could…" I started, but remembered Beatrice and Elizabeth and Mother, and for a second, it was as if my brain was lost in an arctic deep freeze.

"Get a coffee," Lana finished my sentence, her voice light like blue birds on a May morning and her eyes the happy eyes of an eight-year-old entering a carnival for the first time. My fears melted.

"Oh, yes, but maybe if you're not busy, maybe tonight you could come over for dinner." Her joy seemed to evaporate. I realized she had her mother to care for. "Elizabeth, the woman who takes care of my mother, is making a special meal."

"That'd be nice, but I have my mother. You know how it is," Lana said, sounding sorry, as if offering a tender apology.

"You could bring her." I realized after saying this that it was the wrong thing to say to a girl on the first get-together, maybe date. "I mean, if she would like to come, you both could come, if you want." I hoped the growing awkwardness I felt wasn't obvious.

"Jumping cows! Stop talking before you blow this beautiful gift," Max advised. For once, I listened to him and shut up.

"That's sweet. Let me call her. Maybe Mrs. Thorpe, our neighbor, could stay with Mom."

I nodded.

"There's hope for you yet," Max said.

"I better go see the boss," I said.

Van gave me a disapproving look as I neared Mr. Waite's office. "He's been waiting." It was said in Van's well-practiced snob tone, which always made me feel small.

"He looks like a member of the peanut gallery at the gallows," Max sneered. "You deserve better than this." I nodded a thank-you to him.

I gently knocked on Mr. Waite's door. I had a momentary panic, thinking I should have gone to the men's room first and checked my appearance. I had that rotten combination of feeling both unkempt and in trouble.

"Come in," Mr. Waite said. He was standing in front of his ornately carved, dark mahogany desk on his specially designed indoor putting green, a golf putter in hand, a dozen golf balls at his feet, and a frighteningly serious look on his freckled, soft, middle-aged face. Mr. Waite shook his head disapprovingly and made an eight-foot putt. "Two things I really care about, Rodney, two things." He paused, but I did not think it wise to speak. His face grew darker and he croaked, as if this pained him, "Money and golf."

"Yes," I said, trying to sound as if the statement were obvious and he certainly did not need to remind me of it. I anxiously rubbed my palms together and stared at the two richly upholstered wing-backed chairs that formed an alley for his putting green.

Mr. Waite took a few steps and retrieved his ball. He returned to his original spot and leaning on his putter, said, "I just spent the last forty minutes humoring a very pissed-off Roy Buffington." Mr. Waite scowled at me and continued. "He says you scared his wife's dog. The dog is some type of show dachshund, expensive pedigree. Means the world to his wife. Look, I know Beverly Buffington—she's been a well-kept woman all her life. What the hell did you do to the dog? Between telling me what the dog, Caesar, means to the family and how you must have some twisted hatred for canines, I thought Buff was going to cry." Mr. Waite searched my face. "You didn't hear that from me." He lifted his putter and rested it on his shoulder and said with a tone of confidentiality, "So what the hell did you do to Caesar?"

"Nothing. He got scared and ran from Mrs. Buffington. I tried to help. I ended up getting him out from under a counter."

"Your forehead, those are fresh scratches."

"The dog. He clawed me."

Mr. Waite shook his head. "She claims when you bent down to pick up Caesar, which by the way is no name for a runty sausage dog, asking for trouble putting that kind of handle on a squirt. Well, anyway, Bev claims you must have showed your teeth when you were close to her Caesar. She said he was in a weakened state, and you pushed him over the edge. I go way back with Bev and Buff. I can't lose them as customers." Mr. Waite cleared his throat.

"No, of course."

Max shook his head disapprovingly and said, "Tell him the mutt and madam were both doing good when they left."

"When Bev left here, Caesar was still freaking out, according to Buff. Before Beverly could get the dog into her car, he leapt out of her arms onto a fire hydrant and then jumped into a canary-yellow '57 T-bird convertible. The driver, a young lady with braided blond hair, had, according to Buff, some obscenely loud young people's music blaring and did not notice Caesar joining her. Bing-bang. You got the dog one moment, and the next, he's riding off with some stranger enjoying some hip-hop and this beautiful Indian summer weather."

I started to feel like I was going to vomit. "Oh no," I moaned, imagining Mrs. Buffington on the sidewalk in tears as her precious Caesar disappeared, imagining him scaring the crap out of the unsuspecting driver, causing an accident, serious injuries, Caesar taking off on impact, forever lost, lives ruined...all my fault because Max Dowling cannot just go quietly but has to ruin my life before he can rest in peace.

"She knew the car. I guess when she was a kid, her first set of wheels was a '57 T-bird. Her family has old and new money."

"Did she get the license plate number?"

"Right. A vanity plate, L-U-V-U. I'm sure Buff will make a couple of calls, and before dark the police will have Caesar returned home."

I felt relieved.

"The Buffingtons spend a lot of money here. Buff belongs to Whispering Willows Country Club. There's maybe a hundred businessmen who along with other Willows members make up, Van tells me, upward of thirty percent of our business." I could not hide my surprise. "Add in their families, extended families—it's a sizable chunk of dough." Mr. Waite gently guided a ball toward him with his putter. He looked down at the ball, back at me, and then back at the ball and tapped the ball toward the hole on the mat. The ball missed by a hair. "You know Eliot's Fine Men's Clothes? Mitch Eliot is also a member of the club. He has a way of pissing people off. But if word gets around that I've got some kind of weirdo, animal-hating salesman scaring the crap out of little show dogs…you get the picture the way people love their pets."

"I didn't."

Mr. Waite waved his putter in my direction to silence me. "Perceptions become reality. That's what sales are about, right?"

I nodded.

"Tell him that dogs have been taking care of themselves for a million years, so everyone should just take a deep breath and forget about Caesar," Max said, nodding for emphasis.

"I told Buff that we'd talk. Told him how sorry I was and asked if there was anything I could do to help. He seemed okay, but I'm afraid if I don't do something to show how much he and his family mean to me and my business that over time this story will have legs. You know, at the club, and Eliot will make some inroads." Mr. Waite pointed the putter at me again and said with a trace of a smile, "Best defense is a good offense." He nodded and prepared another ball. This time he made the shot. He looked at me, and I gave a slight smile in a way of tribute to his golf skills. "I told Buff if it was all right with him and Bev that you'd call her tonight to find out how they made out with the pooch. Told them I was surprised by all this because you're a dog lover. Lana has their home phone number; you can get it from her."

"Call them tonight." I felt slightly nauseous.

"Right. And, Rodney, if they don't have the dog, you are to tell them that you're worried sick, really heartbroken over their loss. I want you to offer to lead a search to find little Caesar." Mr. Waite looked at me for confirmation, and I grudgingly nodded. "Rodney, if this thing costs me—you know, blows up at the club—I might… hate to say, but I might have to let you go."

I winced.

"Like I said, these folks are connected, and this thing could have legs," Mr. Waite, said.

"Oh fuck me on toast," Max yelled. He stuck his tongue out and pretended to strangle Mr. Waite.

"But I didn't do…"

Mr. Waite raised a hand that silenced me. "Look, most likely they find the dog, he's good, and it blows over. But if not, if my A-list of customers start becoming strangers, if I get icy vibes at the Willows…I'm sorry, but money and golf—you get it."

Max flashed Mr. Waite the bird.

I shook my head.

"You make that call tonight, and let me know where we stand in the morning. Don't look so sad. Better off knowing where you stand than getting blindsided." Mr. Waite spoke with his head down, addressing the ball. He made a putt and, with a hint of a smile, dismissed me.

CHAPTER 10

ALOHA, DR. HITCHFIELD

"A dog shits in your face, and you're getting sacked for it!" Max screamed as we left Mr. Waite's office. "I don't know how you take it. I'm dead, and this prick is killing me. If I were you, I'd get a lawyer. That freckled wormy weasel needs an education, and we should give it to him. I know dozens of ways to rip off businesses." Max jumped, covered his ears, and said, "Sorry, I know, I know, watch and listen."

"Your mother?"

Max nodded.

"I'm good, Max." I tried to reassure him. But I was far from good. I realized at that moment that my time at Haynesworth and Waite's had only been a means to an end. That end was how to pay the bills and eke out what little pleasures the remaining pittance allowed. To the Waites of the world, I was just a replaceable part in a money machine. Max wanted to educate

Mr. Waite—really, I should go in there and thank him because in five short minutes, he had enlightened me regarding my worth to him and his company. I was expendable. I, who had just stared down the barrel of a deranged pimp's revolver; I, who had been saddled with the ghost of my father for the past eighteen hours; I, who had just discovered he could fall for hookers of either sex while pining for the wonderful Lana—it was only fitting that I should end this day by discovering the thing that defined me, my job, was in jeopardy because Max scared a valuable customer's loose-bowelled dachshund. Fine, I thought, nodding to myself and relishing a desire to go back and tell Mr. Waite that I would not be making that call to Mrs. Buffington. But then the idea of telling Mother I got fired flashed before me and chased away all thoughts of rebellion.

I needed Dr. Hitchfield, and thankfully it was time for my appointment.

"You look like shit, kid," Max said.

I nodded and said, "I feel like it too."

"Here comes the boss's eyes and ears," Max said, and gestured with his head toward Van at the front of the store. "Stomp on his toes, hard, and listen for the crunch of bones."

Van approached, wearing a smug look even by Van's standards.

"I've a dentist appointment," I said, and started to walk past him.

"Rodney, that person, was she a friend of yours?" Van asked, with such disgust written over his face you'd think he was in the middle of a pile of manure.

"Person?"

"Yes, the tall, err, black female with the, excuse me, miniskirt, exaggerated nails, and matching heels," Van said, and looked more disturbed with each word he spoke.

"Yes, Van, she's someone who's very special to me."

"Very special?"

"Yes. Wouldn't you say that if someone almost gets you killed that there's a unique relationship that forms between you?"

"Tell him to go fry cheese," Max said.

"Almost killed?"

"Weren't you watching?"

"Watching?"

"Stop repeating my questions."

"Don't take that tone with me."

"I'm taking lunch."

"That special friend," Van's voice became shrill as he continued, "tell her not to come here again. We have a reputation, and streetwalkers are not the clientele we're trying to attract. Tell her if she comes here again, we'll call the police."

"We? Who, you and me?"

"You know what I mean. I'll call the police."

"Right," I said, and kept walking.

As I neared Lana, she gave me a sympathetic smile and said in her sweet, optimistic way, "Mrs. Thorpe can stay with Mother tonight."

"Cancel the shrink, and take this little bundle of joy to lunch," Max said, amazingly without any trace of lechery showing. He then began singing "You Are My Sunshine."

I smiled broadly. "Great, I'll let Mother know. We can leave right from here." Lana nodded. "Lunch," I said, feeling slightly uneasy about deceiving her regarding my destination.

On our way out, Max said, "It could work, Rodney. You and her. I see good things."

"Three years, Max, three years I've been trying to get the courage."

"Rodney, watch yourself; we're in public," Max reminded me, tossing a glance toward an approaching woman in a business suit. "Skip the shrink—you and me should find a safe place to talk, and I'll give you some pointers. You know the longest I ever went without some action was six weeks in 1994. I call it the great slump of '94. I was seeing this Filipino nurse and came down with the flu. Between being sick as a dog and her finding out I made it with her roommate, things ended uglier than a syphilitic warthog. She pretended to care for me, didn't say boo about me and her friend. Being a nurse, she offered me some remedies that would help with the flu. Don't know what she was giving me, but it stole the lead out of my pencil and made me content to watch reruns of *Happy Days*. Then she got tired of slowly poisoning me and let the cat out of the bag. I was pathetic, hobbled by what she was feeding me. I was lucky to escape with my life. As I crawled to my car, she traipsed along with a pair of garden shears, threatening to cut off my bat and balls. Yikes. But I recovered in a week, was back to my old self in two, and since '94 I've been playing a series of extended engagements. I know I can help you. Scoring with the ladies is the only thing I was ever good at."

"Max, this isn't something that will grow or die based on some sleazy line or con."

"Grow or die—I'm talking about you ending up in bed with that little beauty. So get off your high horse, and listen to the master of wine, dine, and lines that gets them in bed."

"Max, listen to me. I care about Lana. I'm not interested in a one-night stand or a relationship based on deception."

Max looked hurt and offered, "Oh. Just trying to help."

"I know."

We walked in silence for a few minutes. I wrestled with how to open my emergency session with Dr. Hitchfield. Do I bring up the stirrings that Beatrice and Dinky sparked? Do I beat around the bush about feelings toward my father with a dead Max standing next to me? Do I bring up my near-death encounter with Spike? Do

I raise my desires for Lana and then introduce Beatrice and Dinky? Do I discuss Ramona Carmello's Italian vacation offer? Do I tell him straight out that I'm losing my mind, that we're not alone?—no, because, you see, Doc, my dead father is right here next to me.

It was like Max read my mind. "Whatever you do, Rodney, don't mention me to this shrink. I'm pretty sure talking ghosts are a guaranteed trip for at least a week in a mental hospital of his choice."

I nodded.

"Good. So what are you going to talk about?"

"I have no idea. But one thing is certain, wherever I start, it will be a fast hour." Max looked at me like he had indigestion. We crossed Main Street and approached the Starr Tower, where Dr. Hitchfield had an office on the eleventh floor.

"You should skip it. You and me could go someplace and talk. I'd like to tell you about my life. I think it's important that you know that I'm more than some low-life who walked out on you and your mother. Wouldn't you like to know about me?"

"Sure, sure, but right now I need Dr. Hitchfield."

"I'm not sure how long I'll be here, and I got a strong feeling that you need to know who I was. See me in a different light."

"For the past eight years, Dr. Hitchfield has kept me sane," I said as patiently as I could. "And today, all of it, from you to Beatrice, Spike, and Caesar…I don't know."

"Your dead father wanting to talk to you, doesn't that trump a little sexual confusion and a near-death experience?"

"Not today," I said, and threw my hands up in frustration.

"Okay, but Lana, you need to get you're A game in place."

Once inside the Starr Tower lobby, there were too many people around for us to talk. Max relentlessly kept telling me to cancel the appointment. "Your only thoughts should be about tonight and Lana."

When I entered Dr. Hitchfield's office, I was greeted by the sound of Don Ho softly singing a Hawaiian love song. In all my visits, music, background or otherwise, had never been heard either in the waiting area or in the good doctor's inner chamber. Max seemed uncomfortable and stared for a few seconds at each of the three large prints that decorated the room: They were abstract works showing subtle changes in the color blue, ranging from a near white to a rich, deep ultra marine. There were four substantial well-cushioned chairs along the wall opposite Dr. Hitchfield's formidable receptionist, Eleanor, who stood as I approached her desk. She was shorter than she sounded. She smiled—the first time I had ever seen her teeth—and in the cheeriest of voices, said, "The doctor will see you shortly, Rodney."

I gave a slight nod and took a seat, thinking how odd Eleanor seemed with her smile and her Don Ho—and where were her typical gray or earth tone dresses? Here she was in a happy, satiny number that jumped to life in a rainbow of colors that formed a pattern of butterflies.

"All things work out for the best," Eleanor mused. In all my years seeing Dr. Hitchfield, the only thing I had ever gotten from Eleanor was "The doctor will see you now" or "Same time next week?"

"Yes," I said, surprised by the comment.

"I mean, you needing to see the doctor today and all."

I scratched my head over my right ear and began to get an uneasy feel. Eleanor's smile seemed to be mocking me. It felt profane.

"I was in the process of calling patients." She giggled and continued, "I started with the less needy ones and was just about ready to call you. You know you never miss. I said, 'That poor'," she hesitated, tilted her head and looked at me as if I were a lost, little boy, "'Rodney Armstrong, he's going to take it hard.'"

"Take it hard?"

"Yes, yes. Good news for Dr. Hitchfield. You won't believe it. I still can't."

"Believe what?" I said, with so much trepidation, I was surprised Eleanor heard me.

"I told you, you should have skipped this expensive hour of bellyaching," Max said, sounding proud of himself.

"He's leaving for Honolulu. The job of his dreams. Taking me with him. Isn't it great!"

"Honolulu, Hawaii?" My stomach hit my knees.

"Honolulu, land of friendly faces and warm embraces."

"What about his patients? Me?"

"Oh, Dr. Palmer Payne is taking over the practice. He's right here on the fifth floor. How convenient. I've never been to Hawaii. Wow!"

I felt cheated and used. I wanted to storm in on the good doctor and let him know what his crazy secretary was telling people.

Eleanor misread me and said, "I always wanted to go. You know, Hawaii is the happiest state in the whole country. I can't believe it. He's paying for everything. He's on cloud nine."

"No!"

"No?" she sounded puzzled but was still smiling from ear to ear.

"He has patients here."

"Tell her tropical beaches and friendly people get old fast," Max said.

"Oh don't worry; it's perfect. Dr. Payne has just relocated from St. Louis and is building up his practice. Perfect. You'll love him. He's so tall, has kind blue eyes. Doesn't look like a psychologist. I joked with him that he was always welcome in the Aloha State."

"She's fried. Slap her silly; knock some sense into her," Max said.

"No, this can't be." My voice cracked, and a tear seeped out the corner of my eye.

"Rodney, please," Eleanor said, through a bright big smile.

"Just like that, no more Dr. Hitchfield."

"Things happen," she nodded. Her smile grew larger.

"Hawaii, no." I shook my head.

"An old college friend, Kermit Sutherland, has all kinds of pull over at Honolulu General. They got together when Kermit was in town a couple of months ago."

"Are you serious?" My chest tightened, and my head felt like a spike had been hammered through my skull.

"Kermit offered Dr. Hitchfield a senior position, with the kind of perks you can't even imagine. It's a once-in-a-life-time opportunity. He's tired of the winters here." Eleanor sighed and then began to do a hula and danced around her chair. "Not in a million years did I think anything like this would ever happen. Aren't you happy for us?" She contentedly rested her plump chin on her raised folded hands.

My stomach felt like I was trying to digest rocks. My blood pumped like a boxer ready to slug it out for ten rounds. Violence crossed my mind so strongly that it scared me out the door. Eleanor called to me, but I was too upset to hear what she said and kept walking.

Max chased behind me gleefully. "What the hell kind of doctor is he?"

Fear of crying kept me from answering. I imagined Dr. Hitchfield in a Hawaiian shirt, sipping an exotic drink. How could he? I could tell Max was trying to soothe me, but I couldn't hear what he was saying. It wasn't until we reached the bench outside the courthouse on Main Street that I heard him say, "The first time I ran away from home was when I was twelve."

I sat down on the bench and said, "I never thought it would end like this. I should go back and give him a piece of my mind. I don't know, Max. I feel so…"

"Made it to Hartford; two hippies in a beat-up Chevy Corvair picked me up. First time I ever smoked pot. Everything is better when you're twelve—or worse, depending on what happens next."

"I feel so…" I couldn't say it, alone.

"Connecticut State Police turned me over to the Massachusetts State Police."

"Max, I'm trying to figure something out here that is critical."

"When you're twelve, cops are very cool."

"Can you just listen to me, Max?" I hollered, and four attorney types, wearing the weight of the world, gave me the strangest look as they headed into the courthouse.

"Shush," Max said, pressing a finger to his lips.

"Dr. Hitchfield was my certainty, my anchor. All week, every week, when it was getting too much with Mother or work, I'd think of Dr. Hitchfield, and I'd know I could do it. I could make it. I could handle whatever life threw at me. You see how big this is?"

"Sonny boy, that ship is sailing to Hawaii."

I cringed and whimpered, "I needed him badly, today of all days."

"You need to forget about that little shit bird Caesar, forget about those hookers, forget about that ugly bastard who tried to kill you, forget about your boss, forget about your mother, forget about me, and think about Lana, Lana, Lana."

"What if Waite fires me?"

"Then he's crazier than he looks. But like I said, forget about him too."

I heard a car door close and looked up. Slick was leaning against Jags Carmello's Lincoln, his eyes hiding behind wraparound sunglasses. Coming toward me was that mountain of a man, Bruno, who, unbelievably, looked small next to his companion, a walking wall in a black silk suit coat, well-creased charcoal pants, and Slick's style of sunglasses. Panicking, I flashed back to my morning interactions with Ramona. Bruno must have told Jags that that smart salesman was hitting on Ramona. And now, they were going to kill me. "Max," I croaked, and pointed a trembling finger at the approaching monsters.

"The goombas have landed," Max said as they neared.

"Shit, Max, this isn't funny." Cold sweat covered me.

The larger man moved ahead of Bruno. I mumbled a chant of "Oh shit…" The larger man put a big, heavy foot, the kind of foot that could crush a face as if it were made of straw, on the bench next to me. Would he shoot me or snap my neck?

"Stay cool," Max advised.

Bruno cleared his throat and almost apologetically said, "The boss needs to see you."

On impulse I dropped to the ground, clutched Bruno's knees, and began to beg, "Please, please, don't kill me. I've got a sick mother. Please. This is all a big misunderstanding."

Bruno grabbed my underarm and lifted me to my feet. "Kill you?"

"That's not why you're here? I'm under a lot of stress. The pressure is killing me. And I don't know what I'm doing."

"I thought you was fucked up. I mean, we're watching, and you're sitting here talking to yourself," Bruno said, patting my shoulders as if trying to straighten me out.

"So much has happened, Bruno," I said, trying to stop my shaking.

"Tough day," Bruno said.

"They wouldn't kill you out in the open like this. Just don't go anywhere with them." Max cautioned, shaking his head disapprovingly.

"I just thought—I don't know."

"I told you, Chops," Bruno said to his companion, who lowered his foot from the bench. "You have a menacing presence."

My legs were noticeably shaking, and Chops said, "Relax, kid." It was said in a raspy growl. A voice not used to verbal arguments or offering explanations. He motioned to the bench, and I sat down. "You thought we's going whack you." Chops spit out a laugh and rubbed my head as if I was a ten-year-old.

"You blew it," Max said. "You've introduced the idea. It's like waving red meat in front of a hungry wolf." He made a slashing motion across his neck. "With these guys you have to play it cool. I know that's asking a lot, but act like your life depends on it."

I was too scared to be bothered by Max.

Bruno and Chops looked down at me. I could see pity in Bruno's eyes and a noncommittal black glare from Chops's sunglasses. "You taking something for your nerves?" Bruno asked.

"Not in a while," I said.

"Probably shouldn't have stopped," Bruno said.

My breathing began to return to normal.

"The boss needs to see you," Bruno repeated.

"Me?" I was still shaking and not certain if I had said anything wrong to Ramona.

Bruno nodded. "All hell broke out."

"He didn't like the shirts?" I posed meekly.

Chops slapped my shoulder and almost knocked me off the bench. "This kid's a riot, a real fucking riot. Didn't like the shirts."

Bruno then said, dead seriously, "Mrs. Carmello wants you to go to Italy with them." He shook his head and with sleepy gentle eyes, said, "She told the Boss that you know Italy like you was born there. She went on and on about the places you told her about."

"Go with it, Rodney," Max said.

"I'm flattered, but…" I started.

"Listen, kid, you don't know what you started," Bruno said.

"Started?"

"The boss looks at the clothes and says, 'What's wrong with what I always wear? It's a good thing she didn't get him the yellow one," Bruno said.

"'You look like an undertaker,' Mrs. Carmello screams at the boss," Chops interjected.

"Then she goes on and on about him not wanting to go to Italy in the first place," Bruno said, and gave a shrug. "From there it went downhill. The boss starts with as long as he's paying the bills around here, he'll decide where he goes and what he wears. Mrs. Carmello counters with how she doesn't have to hear this crap."

"I don't see how this involves me," I said, trying to be assertive without pissing anyone off.

"It was World War Three, kid," Chops said, sitting next to me. The closeness of his enormous bulk told me that whatever they wanted would happen.

"Correct," Bruno said, and nodded as if that explanation should be sufficient.

"They've been married a long time; couples fight," I offered.

"The boss has a rule: men don't hit women. Mrs. Carmello wouldn't let it go. She kept saying she wasn't going to spend three weeks in Italy watching him drink grappa and check out *puttane.* She said if you went with her, they could see all the sights and Boss could get drunk and get lost with some Roman bimbo. Never thought anybody would talk to the boss like that. She really, I don't now…" Bruno paused.

"Got under his skin," Chops said, and nodded knowingly.

"Correct," Bruno said.

"So ba-ba-boom," Chops said, and slapped his left palm with his right hand with such force that I winced.

"Mrs. Carmello, after she got off the floor, started talking about cutting the boss's throat when he was sleeping." Bruno sounded truly sorry about the whole situation.

"It freaking snowballed. I never saw the boss so mad. I says to myself, 'Just keep your mouth shut, Ramona.' Thankfully she did," Chops said.

"Boss went outside to cool off. Mrs. Carmello packed her bags, took two jewelry cases. Had me load everything into her Mercedes, and off she went," Bruno told me, shaking his head. "Boss figures if he shows how sorry he is and, you know, has you going with us to Italy and all, she'll forgive him."

"This is your ticket out of being Waite's doormat!" Max cried, excitedly.

"Maybe he should wait her out," I said again, trying to be diplomatic.

"She ran over to Little Jags's," Chops stated, as if that knocked my idea out of the ballpark.

"Little Jags?"

"The kid is something. Smartest kid you'd ever want to meet," Bruno boasted proudly.

"Book smart," Chops said dismissively.

"He went to college in New York," Bruno said.

"And all those uppity fag professors turned him into what?" Chops said, letting out a massive wad of spit. He folded his arms and made a face, as if the thought of Little Jags was a lot for him to handle.

"Studied a lot of sociology," Bruno said. "He told me at his graduation party that we are the products of both our personal and our larger environmental experiences. We need to change both if we see they're a problem. I told him I had no problems other than it's hard to get, as you know, suits off the rack that fit."

"It turned him into a crybaby. How we should feel sorry for all those bums who got their hands out begging all the time," Chops said disgustedly. Then he raised a hand as if he and Bruno had some heated history over the topic.

"I think we need do-gooders, just not living with us," Bruno said, directing this to Chops, who sighed. "Well, anyway, Little Jags is living in Boston. He left all this to work at a home for troubled kids."

"That's what's wrong with this country. Used to be, trouble either got you ready for life, or it wrecked you. Now it's everybody's problem if you got problems. All these crybabies are killing this country," Chops complained.

"Chops always had a soft spot for Little Jags," Bruno said.

"The kid used to love being with me. When he was little he'd spend the whole time at the Columbus Day parade on my shoulders," Chops reminisced.

"He's turned his back on all of us, like we're..."

"Dirt," Chops interrupted.

Max began singing, "Arrivederci, Rodney, goodbye, goodbye for now..."

"So Mrs. Carmello has gone to stay with Little Jags," Bruno said.

"She knows nobody will contact the kid," Chops said.

"But anyway, you need to talk to the boss," Bruno said.

I looked at my watch and said, "I got to be back at work in like ten minutes."

"Don't worry about it," Bruno said.

"I need this job," I insisted.

"The boss doesn't like to be disappointed, and I'm not disappointing him," Chops said, and laid a hand that felt like a sack of potatoes on my shoulder.

"I screwed up today at work, and I can't just blow off the rest of the day."

"Is it going to kill you?" Chops asked.

His question came as a threat, and all of my original fears of them executing me came roaring back. In a muffled mousy voice, I said, "Hope not."

"The boss will call your boss. It's going to be fine," Bruno assured me.

Chops took me by the upper arm, and lifted me off the bench. Bruno started walking toward Slick, who opened the Lincoln's back door. Chops effortlessly guided me in next to Bruno like the tide depositing seashells on the beach. Then he and Slick climbed in up front. Max slipped in between me and Bruno, looking awestruck as Tony Bennett sang "Smile" on the stereo system. As the car pulled away, Max said, "What a quality sound. Lush. That's what it is, Rodney, lush."

CHAPTER 11

TEA FOR TWO

Bruno sat back in his seat like a man at peace with the world and asked, "Rodney, you like sausage and peppers?"

I sighed and shook my head no. Food was a million miles away as visions of an angry Jags grew uglier and uglier. Then Jags's face morphed into an image of Mr. Waite firing me with the ease of making a two-foot putt.

"You see that dial? It controls the sound back here," Max said, smiling as if he were having a grand old time. "And this, Rodney," he pointed to a panel, "this controls the temperature. You cool enough?"

I gave Max a look of what I thought was disdain but he mistook it for climate discomfort. "Go ahead, set the temperature the way you like it. Ask him if you can change it; go ahead." I shook my head. "Suit yourself;

the great thing about my present condition, I'm never hot or cold. Hope it stays this way. How's the ride?"

"Jags's mom brought over a pan of sausage, peppers, and mushrooms. Enough to feed an army," Bruno said, poking me in the side with his elbow. "Jags's brother, Frankie, owns Francesco's Restaurant over on Broadhurst. Great cooks, Frankie and the old lady. Frankie's specialties are desserts and cream sauces. I get hungry just thinking about it. He made a cream cake for Jags's birthday last month. The thing was a foot high, loaded with peaches, cherries. Chops, wasn't that some cake?"

"Frankie's the best," Chops said. "We's just getting ready to dig into the sausage and peppers. Jags was slicing some bread when the fireworks started." He turned toward me. "Freaking World War Three."

"I think if we had started eating before you going to Italy had come up, it would have been a very different story," Bruno said.

"Everything sounds better when you're digging into something delicious. Even some real shit isn't so bad on a full gut," Chops agreed. "That's why they give guys a feast for their last meal. Figure even dying is better when your belly's full."

My cell phone rang. I looked over at Bruno and spied the number on the screen. "It's home," I said.

"Go ahead. Just don't say where's you going or who's you with," Bruno said, and winked, not in a playful way but as if to make sure I understood.

I inhaled deeply and said, "Hello." I could feel distress in my voice.

"Mr. Rodney, I am so sorry to bother you at your work, but do you know this woman's not a very good woman?"

"Calm down, Elizabeth."

"I cannot calm down. I am so angry. Do you know why?"

"Please, Elizabeth, calm down."

"This woman, Beatrice, she comes here dressed like a street person."

"Street person?"

"What do you call a woman who sells her body? I don't want to sound rude."

"No, it's streetwalker."

"Sounds good, Rodney boy," Bruno chuckled.

"All right, streetwalker. If that's not bad enough, she is high as a kite. Talking nonsense of how you saved her from certain death. How you faced down her man who was going to kill the two of you. Your mother told her to find the rest of her skirt and come back when she is decent."

"What did Beatrice do?"

"Laughed and said she has to wait here until you came home. She's talking a mile a minute. Said it's not safe for her on the streets. That Spike somebody was still on the loose."

"That's true, Elizabeth. I told her I would help her."

"Your mother wanted to call the police; Beatrice told her she would take her chances out on the streets. Your mother was fine with that, but then this Beatrice started sobbing, saying such kind things about you. Your mother began to soften that's when I was ready to call the police. I told your mother, let me call you instead. Beatrice said you would set us straight. Then she went into this long story. Your mother has changed like a hurricane that moves out to sea and you catch sunshine instead of a killer storm. I said let me call you, I'm not buying what she is selling. I'm in the bathroom for privacy. What should we do?"

"She needs my help. I trust her, Elizabeth."

"But you know what she does for a living?" There was pained panic in Elizabeth's voice.

"Yes." I felt my head was about to explode.

"I don't understand," Elizabeth said, as if she had heard wrong. "You said nothing. You tell us nothing; we are to do what? I can't believe it. Your mother thinks you have cracked up."

"I didn't think it was a big deal," I said, looking at Bruno, who had his eyes glued on me.

"This woman told us wild tales of guns and you saving her life. It is not my place, but how on this good earth did you get involved with her?"

"It's a long story."

"Your mother asked, and she told us you were so upset about work that you absentmindedly walked into her and knocked her coffee out of her hand. That you bought her another coffee, gentleman that you are, but her man got angry because he suspected you of wanting sex with her. Did you?"

"No."

"She said he got angry because between her and this other street person—streetwalker—they should have made you happy."

"No, her man has mental problems and thought I wanted sex with her, but I would never do that."

Bruno gave me a strange look.

"Your mother now has hopes that you can reform this woman. She told her since getting to know me, she's good with black people. I think she meant this as a compliment. This Beatrice started picking up on your mother wanting you to find someone, and she is playing on your mother feeling sorry for her while building you up as some kind of superman. I don't know how it changed from calling the police to her feeling sorry for her. My head is spinning, but here I am calling you."

"What happened?"

"Your mother's eyes changed in how she looked at Beatrice. She is beginning to worry me. I think she thinks you and this woman are, you know, a thing."

"It's nothing like that. But Beatrice has been through a lot."

"Don't deceive yourself; if she wants to go out like that and do those things, then she has only herself to thank for any problems. I never. This is very bad."

"Please, just make her feel welcome."

"Your mother now is all smiles. Telling her how she loves Martin Luther King and Denzel Washington. Laughing, and not that little mean laugh she makes when someone has screwed up."

"They're getting along?"

"Famously—it makes me want to throw her skinny ass out the window. I smell trouble, big, big trouble."

"Do this for me, please, Elizabeth."

"Of course I will, but I need your help; this is too much. You need to come home."

"I'm kind of busy."

There was a long pause, and then Elizabeth sounded apologetic. "I'm sorry to bother you, I just needed to let it out. I'm afraid she'll rob you or your mother. That her friends will show up and rob you. I know this kind— big trouble, Mr. Rodney. They're always scheming. You would be better with a house full of snakes than one such as this Beatrice."

"I'll try to get home as soon as I can, but I may be late."

"I will do my best for you and your mother."

"Thanks. Are you sure Mother is okay with her?"

"Yes, yes. I made a pot of tea. They're in the kitchen sipping tea and eating butter cookies. Your mother is beaming."

"She knows Beatrice is a prostitute?"

"Yes, she told us the problems with her man and everything. But you are not interested in her or anything?"

"No, I just want to help her. Felt bad about her life, but I have no interest in her," I whispered, and noticed Bruno's eyebrow rose again and his nose wrinkled.

"I'm in the bathroom. I should get back out there. I don't trust her."

"I think she's okay."

"Excuse me, Mr. Rodney, but how long have you known her?"

"Not long."

"How long?"

"Five or six hours," I mumbled.

"Five or six months?"

"No, hours," I meekly repeated.

"Hours!" Elizabeth screamed.

"Yes, hours. But I have a good feeling about her."

"Forgive me, Mr. Rodney, but if you think you can change someone like that, you are making a big mistake. I'm afraid for you and your mother. I think you should come home. She's talking like you are her savior. About how she was trapped and frightened but now she knows she can face anything. Your mother kept asking, 'This is my Rodney you're talking about?' This tramp said you were one-in a million, a lifesaver. Then your mother asked if she wanted tea and cookies."

"Tea?"

"Yes. They are all nicey-nice. She is telling us that she is leaving for Baltimore and probably never coming back. Your mother asked her what was the big attraction in Baltimore. She said family and a new start. Your mother pressed for details. She said that it's complicated and that you could explain it later. I gave her a look that told her I'm not buying it. I believe she is setting you up to steal from you. She didn't like the way I was looking at her. She changed the subject back to you and how good and special you are. Your mother's eyes are big and smiling. She has the look of the marrying mother."

"Marrying mother?"

"Yes, when a mother has given up on the idea of her child marrying and giving them grandchildren. Then when a possible mate arrives at their door, within minutes in their head, they are planning a wedding. They do not know this, but they are. It's as if they are hypnotized."

"Mother? Are you sure?"

"Yes, I know that look. She is even overlooking the fact this woman is a streetwalker. Have there been no girlfriends, Mr. Rodney?"

"Girlfriends?" I laughed and said, "Not in years."

"But you and she are not…"

"No, Elizabeth, I just want to help her. I have no interest in something like that."

Bruno shook his head.

"You sound like you're gay," Max said.

I shrugged and asked Elizabeth, "Has Mother been drinking?"

"No, but she is getting drunk with the idea of you and this Beatrice."

"Maybe her oxygen tank is low."

"No, it is the idea of her boy finding a woman."

"I don't believe it."

"Believe it. Your mother either feels you will never find anyone and will settle for anyone, even a prostitute, or she thinks you are crazy and hopes maybe a woman, any woman, will straighten you out. Part of your mother worries that you are—now don't get mad—gay."

I imagined me and Dinky. I snapped in defense, "I'm not gay."

"No, you just haven't asked a girl out since high school and got excited today over a young hustler with a pair of balls," Max said. He then buried his head into my side and raised his right arm as if warding off an attack.

"I believe you," Elizabeth said.

"Sorry. I didn't mean to bite off your head just don't know why she'd think that."

"Come home. I don't know what will happen next. She said she has to wait for you, and I'm afraid I may let my feelings out, and that I'm sure will be bad."

"Please, Elizabeth, she's my guest."

"Hurry home."

"I'll try, but it's very busy. Oh, can we feed one more person tonight?"

"Not her?"

"No, Lana from work. I invited her; she's very nice. Will there be enough?"

"Not like this one?"

"No, nothing like Beatrice."

"When will you be here?"

"Not sure, maybe around seven."

"Please hurry; I am starting to prepare our feast, and somehow it seems very wrong with her sitting with her long legs crossed like an evil trap sipping tea with your mother."

The conversation ended. Bruno sank deeper in his seat, tapped gently on his armrest, and said, almost sweetly, "You like guys?"

"No, no, no," I protested.

"What's the big deal? I saw this video—Chops, what was that video called?"

"What video?"

"The one where the broads were getting off on a boa constrictor." Bruno laughed, slapped my shoulder playfully, and added, "No shit, a real snake. You should have seen these broads. What was that video Chops?"

"Who the fuck remembers?" Chops said.

"I'm thinking Mrs. Carmello figured you out. Figured you're safe traveling with her you know, the boss will have fewer problems you being with her, knowing you like the boys. She always said you were a sweet guy, a gentleman. Maybe that's code for gay," Bruno said, gently shaking my shoulder as if to show his tolerance.

"Broads can spot you fags a mile away," Chops said.

"I'm not gay."

"No, but what I could make out, you got a friend over to your place who is a pro and wanted to have sex and you turned her down, and you haven't had a girl in a long time, right?" Bruno said.

I stared blankly at him.

"That's what I got from what you said," Bruno said.

"I got no use for you gay bastards," Slick piped in from behind the steering wheel.

"This kid's harmless," Chops said.

"They're killing this country. It's a bigger problem than you think," Slick said.

"Maybe they are, but Rodney here comes across, you know…" Bruno started but didn't finish as we pulled into Jags's driveway.

"I'm not gay."

"Play this right, and you could be sitting pretty," Max whispered to me.

"If Joey Fangs or Fat Freddy are there, don't let on about being gay," Chops said. "Very narrow-minded. They hate gays, just like this one here." He motioned with his head toward Slick. "Only they got anger-management issues."

As we were getting out of the car, Bruno said, "One thing I got to know, aren't you worried about AIDS?"

"I'm not gay."

"Whatever, but your end of the conversation and your way, don't get me wrong, has gay shit written all over it," Bruno said, shaking his head as he held the door open for me.

CHAPTER 12

THE PIZZA MAN

"Look at those columns, and all that stonework. You know what it costs to have a walkway like that?" Max asked in awe, admiring the entrance to Jags's palatial Tudor-style estate.

"Shit, look who's here," Slick said, alerting Chops and Bruno. His eyes narrowed at the house's front door as if expecting a world of trouble. He felt his right calf as he slowly walked toward the house.

"He's checking for his piece," a giddy Max said, sounding like a kid who couldn't believe what he was seeing. "You see, Rodney, that's what separates guys like us from guys like them. They know it's dangerous, yet they're drawn to it by some powerful desire to show guys like us that they're the real deal."

Chops touched his side, silently communicating for Bruno to look toward the circular driveway's right. There was a black Cadillac with the license plate PIZZAMN. The nose of the car was pushed against the start of a line of well-manicured, four-foot-high shrubs. Bruno opened the car's passenger side door and retrieved a small handgun from the glove compartment. "Stay here," Bruno said as he started toward the house, holding his gun close to his shoulder.

"Feels like a movie," Max said.

"And I'm the only one who doesn't know his part," I whispered and began to slink away from the house toward the quiet residential street with its acre lots of million-dollar homes.

"Hey, swish, where the hell are you going?" Slick called.

I pretended not to hear and kept walking. I was too scared to look anywhere but straight ahead. I imagined if I made it to the road, thirty yards away, I had a chance of not dying or witnessing whatever had turned Slick, Chops, and Bruno into Jags's frighteningly cautious, dangerously armed protectors.

"Shit, fuck," Slick moaned.

I thought of running, but an image of me lying face down with my brains splattered in the driveway caused my legs to slow. I considered zigzagging my way to safety—Slick firing at a zig just as I zagged—but I was certain I would zig into a bullet.

"Don't look now, but we got company," Max said.

I heard Slick's racing footfalls and then his right hand grabbed my left arm above the elbow. His grip was surprisingly strong. He spun me around and snarled, "Where do you think you're going?"

"Tell him you didn't want to be a bother. Whatever you do, don't appear too weak or too strong. These alpha dogs can blow like Vesuvius if they're challenged or go for the kill if they smell blood," Max said.

"Looked like a bad time for company," I said. My teeth chattered like when I venture out on frosty mornings without a jacket.

"We'll wait here," Slick said.

I nodded, noticing the handle of a pistol protruding above his belt. Max and I looked at each other. "Now's a good time for prayers," Max said, and he began mumbling something.

Chops and Bruno were now inside the mansion, a sprawling affair that looked as if it were large enough to be having a quiet lunch at one end and an execution at the other with the participants of both being unaware of the existence of the other.

"Relax, Rodney," Slick said.

"Act like you haven't noticed the gun or the PIZZA plate," Max said.

"This seems like a bad time to talk with Mr. Carmello," I said, and was pleasantly surprised by my relative calm.

"Just business. Bruno went in to find out what's up. Don't want to disturb the boss." Slick yawned and said, "Let's go wait by the car." He waved his hand toward the Lincoln, and I reluctantly led the way.

"Pick up a rock and smash in his head. Take his gun and drive off. It's your best shot at not joining me. Because if it hasn't already happened, very soon something terrible is going to happen in that place," Max said, motioning toward Jags's house. He continued apologetically, "Rodney, I'm sorry for running out on you. I wish I had known you when you were a kid."

"Thanks," I muttered, half to myself.

"What did you say?" Slick asked, resting his behind on the passenger side of the Lincoln.

"I can't afford to lose my job."

"Jags and your boss are like this," Slick said, raising a crossed index and middle finger.

I wiped sweat from my forehead.

"My father ran out on us, too," Max said. "My mother, your grandmother, had a string of lowlife boyfriends. She always went from bad to worse."

"Jags is probably doing some business. Come over here—I don't feel like yelling," Slick motioned with his chin for me to stand next to him. I complied.

A voice inside me said to keep my eyes off the PIZZAMN's car. And like when you're told not to think of a red apple and then that's all you can think of, my eyes kept darting back to the black Caddy.

"I can see I just repeated the same rotten mistakes my old man did, and I'm sorry, Rodney. If I could do it over, I'd try to settle down."

"It's okay," I said, and I could hear my emotions ready to run wild.

Slick gave me a troubled look.

"It's okay if I'm late for work. I know Mr. Carmello is a busy man."

"It's good you understand. You know how Jags makes his money?" Slick asked.

I shook my head no, suppressing recent accounts that were provided by the district attorney for the newspapers of the disturbing tentacles of Anthony "Jags" Carmello's powerful crime organization. According to the DA, Jags made his money from loan sharking, dealing a wide assortment of illegal drugs, shipping stolen high-end cars to Europe and the Middle East, hijacking big-ticket items out of several New England ports and air terminals, and worming his way into several legitimate local businesses.

Max stood beside me and wrapped his weightless spirit arms around me. "You turned out good. Uptight but good. I only wish I knew you before. Do you like to fish?" Max was swept up with emotion and dropped his masked face onto my shoulder.

Tears began to roll down my cheeks.

Fortunately Slick was focusing on the house's front door as he began to explain Jags's fortune. "He's an entrepreneur—big name for businessman. He's got a restaurant, a package store, and a dry cleaner's. All that talk in the newspapers is just talk. You see, the boss got off in court. The DA coming after Jags is good politics. That's all it is, Rodney. If his name was Smith or Jones, you wouldn't know he existed. It's all a lot of nonsense—makes me sick." Slick turned to me and barked, "You crying!"

"Allergies," I said, and pulled out my handkerchief. I wiped my eyes and blew my nose.

"Never saw a guy out of the blue start bawling," Slick said.

I shrugged and said, "They come on fast."

"I almost came back here about ten years ago. I knew I had a kid, but I wasn't man enough to try to make things right. Now it's too late," Max said.

"It's okay," I blubbered.

"You're really bawling," Slick said.

"Tell him you're scared," Max said.

"I'm scared."

"Scared? I thought you had allergies."

"I do, but it's all the drama, the guns."

"Precautions, that's what Bruno gets paid to do. He's Mr. Careful." Slick let out a most disingenuous laugh.

"These guys are missing the sympathy gene," Max said.

I ran my dry tongue over my drier lips, thought to myself, The hell with it, and let out what I was thinking. "I know Jags's reputation and the way you guys acted getting out of the car. I'm sure the Pizza Man is one of your, eh, problems, and I know how you deal with problems."

"What the hell? Are you nuts? That's Vinnie Pizza's car, and as sure as I'm talking to you, he's fine and dandy talking to the boss. Shit, when this is over, I'll take you over to Vinnie's Pizzeria and buy you a slice, and you, me, and the Pizza Man will have a laugh at your expense. You've been watching too many movies."

While Slick was talking, Max repeatedly asked me to forgive him.

"Yes, of course," I said.

"Thanks, son," Max said, fighting back ghost tears.

"That's the problem with guys like you—you believe Hollywood," Slick said. As he spoke, our attention was drawn to the front door.

Bruno came out hollering to Slick, "Take him round back to the kitchen."

"It's easier to kill a 'him' than a Rodney," Max said.

"I really need to call work," I said nervously.

"After you talk to the boss, one of us will take you back. Wipe your eyes. The boss will get a kick out of your imagination."

"Act like you know nothing, and agree to every-thing," Max cautioned.

"Come on," Slick said, and led the way past Vinnie Pizza's Cadillac to a side door. The door was locked, and Slick rapped gently and then, after a few seconds, with more force. The kitchen entrance was out of view from the front entrance. From its bottom step, where I was standing, if I turned my head back toward the front entrance, I could see the black Cadillac's rear quarter. A voice inside me told me not to turn toward the Caddy. I unfortunately did not heed that voice. I looked back as

Slick began to rap on the door for a third time. It was only a glance, but I'm sure fifty years from now, I'll still remember what I saw as clearly as the moment my eyes caught sight of them. Bruno, his back toward me, supervised a short man who was built like a dumpster and a tall wiry man with salt-and-pepper-colored hair and a dark complexion. The two men were depositing a rolled-up carpet into the trunk of the Pizza Man's Cadillac. The carpet was not so long that it should require two men to carry it—unless Vinnie Pizza's dead body was wrapped inside it.

Chops, out of breath, opened the door for us. "Come on in, the boss is having coffee. What can I get you, Rodney?"

"I'm good."

"You sure? Because there's a nice spice cake. Doesn't that sound good, coffee and cake? You don't look so hot. A nice cup of mud and some cake will do you right," Chops said, giving a toothy grin that was almost kindly.

"No, I got to get back to work."

The kitchen was an open twenty-by-twenty-foot space. Walnut cabinets to the ceiling occupied the side opposite the massive stainless steel refrigerator and a six-burner gas stove. Cream-colored tiles with tiny rosettes covered the walls, and larger complementary but darker tiles made up the floor. Across the kitchen was an informal dining area that had a wall of windows overlooking a flower garden bursting with yellow and white mums. In the garden's center was a white marble fountain with a maiden figure dressed in classical Roman attire holding a large urn from which water poured. Jags sat facing us as we entered. He was dressed in a navy-blue polo shirt and well-pressed gray pants. His curly dark-brown hair was cut short. He looked like a man at home enjoying a day off, relaxing with coffee and cake. "Rodney, it's so good to see you," Jags said, lifting his cup as if to salute me. He then told Slick to get me something to eat.

"I'm good," I repeated.

"Don't refuse him on the little things. Don't need to go out of your way to offend a man who rolls up his problems in carpets that are never seen again," Max whispered.

"What the hell happened to your head?"

"A customer's dog; it's a long story," I said, and jammed my hands into my armpits for a second.

"No way, a dog?" Jags said.

"A little dachshund; it got scared and jumped on my head."

"That's funny, a little mutt on your head, right there in the middle of Haynesworth and Waite's. That's something I'd like to see." He laughed, and Chops and Slick laughed with him. "Looks like you've been picking at pimples. Son of a bitch, a little mutt did that. You kill it?"

My eyes widened.

"Don't tell me, you didn't even kick the mutt into next week?"

"Make something up," Max said.

I shook my head no.

When Jags stopped talking, Slick whispered something in his ear. I assumed it was about my thoughts concerning Jags's problem-resolution strategies. "Sit down; have some coffee," Jags said kindly.

"How do you like your coffee?" Slick asked.

"Light with one sugar," I said, taking a seat across from Jags, thinking Max was right. I needed to keep this light and friendly, even though all I wanted was to run out the door and keep running until my heart burst or Slick shot me.

"My wife tells me you're an expert on Italy," Jags said.

"I wouldn't say expert."

"Don't be modest. We're going for three weeks. I've never been out of the country. That's not true. I've been to Canada, but it doesn't feel foreign. My wife has been planning this for years. She's got brochures coming out the ying-yang. It means so much to her, so it's important to me. You know, you want to keep the wife happy." Jags laughed.

Slick put a cup of coffee down next to me, along with a three-inch-wide slice of cake. I nodded a thank-you.

"My wife made the cake yesterday. She's a great baker. If she'd made it today, I'd have my enemies taste it first," Jags said, and started laughing. Chops and Slick didn't join him; they both shifted their eyes momentarily away from their boss. I assumed Mrs. Carmello was a very touchy subject. When Jags stopped laughing, he said in a frighteningly serious voice, "I've got a big problem, and I believe you're the guy who can fix it."

"Me?" I gulped.

"My wife thinks you're the sweetest guy there is. Whenever she comes back from your place, it's always 'Rodney this' and 'Rodney that.' Make a guy jealous." Jags gave a dismissive chuckle and continued, "I always liked you, and that thing you got for the boys, that's okay."

"Mr. Carmello, I'm not gay."

"You know, my man Bruno, he says different. And Bruno, not like Slick there, is slow to form an opinion. You can go to the bank with what Bruno tells you." I turned my head toward the windows behind Jags. "Hey, I didn't mean to insult you. Whatever you are as long as you leave me and mine alone, I couldn't care less."

"Mr. Carmello, I really need to get back to work."

"Don't worry about Waite. I already called him. Told him I needed to see you. Told him we're in need of your expertise. I told Waite I'd pay you for your time. He wanted to know if I was going to the country club soon; he wants to buy me a drink. So relax, Rodney. It's all good."

"He's lying. You see how his eyes shifted when he said he'd pay you?" Max said.

"Look, Mr. Carmello—"

"Call me Jags. I want you to be Ramona's personal tour guide when we're in Italy—all expenses paid. You'd be our personal guest. Whatever you want, you got. I think having somebody like you explaining things to my wife, making sure she's okay, would really make for a wonderful trip for her. And to be honest, it would make my time there better too."

"I'm honored, but afraid I can't."

"Can't?" It was said with great surprise, as if my joining him, Ramona, and Bruno on their Italian excursion was a foregone conclusion in Jags's mind.

"I've got my mother to care for."

"We'll take her with us," Jags said, and smiled a reassuring smile.

"She's not well, and a trip like that would be too much." It occurred to me that a trip like that would kill her, and I could thank Jags for no more Mother. A smile crept across my face, and I immediately was seized with guilt.

"What's so funny?" Jags asked.

"Nothing."

"Nothing, you started smiling. You thinking maybe you could do this, maybe a free trip to Italy sounds good?"

"Besides Mother, I've got so much going on here. Thank you, but I can't."

"Rodney, whatever it is, let me help you. I know if I tell Ramona you're coming with us, she'd be the happiest woman alive. You see, me and Ramona had words, and right now it'd mean a lot if I made her happy."

"I'm sure you can hire someone there to take you on a private tour."

"It's not the same. You know me. You know Ramona. We trust you."

"Be strong, son," Max said.

"About that gay shit, don't worry about it. I couldn't care less what you are, as long as you show respect, who cares?"

"No, it's not that; it's—it's everything. Me being here, and everything." I looked around and threw my hands up.

"Being here?" Jags asked.

"I had my day planned, and coming here wasn't part of it."

"Careful, Rodney," Max advised.

Jags shrugged and said, "They didn't rough you up, did they?"

"No, but I didn't think I had a choice in going with them."

"Everybody's got a choice. Like me, I can throw my marriage away after thirty years or try to get my Ramona back. I'm going to do whatever I can to get her back, and I think you, my friend, are the key for that to happen."

"So what you want is all that matters?"

"To me, it's the most important thing, but it's not everything. Just like for you, I'm sure what you want is most important."

"But you go to extremes to get what you want."

"Extremes?"

"Yes, like thinking I could drop everything and go with you to Italy just because you really don't want to spend your days seeing art and religious treasures. That I could be a traveling companion for your wife while you and Bruno have a great old time hanging around a bar or whatever."

"Where's the harm in that?"

"You have a marriage. Your wife wants a special trip with you, not me."

"Wrong. She knows me and knows she'd have a better time in those churches and museums with you. It was her idea."

"But you should be willing to sacrifice a little to make her happy."

"I'm sacrificing more than ten g's already for this trip."

"Well, sorry, but you need to find someone else. Don't you have a relative or friend who is interested and would love a free trip?"

"The only guy I know is my brother-in-law. He's been to Italy a dozen times, speaks the language. He loves the place—should stay there."

"Perfect."

"Perfect for him, but three days with his big mouth, and one of us would be dead, and it wouldn't be me. Never mind three weeks."

"That's what I'm talking about. There's this overlay of violence."

"You're too sensitive."

"Even coming here. I felt like I had no choice."

"I'm sorry. Sometimes my guys get a little carried away."

"I still feel uncomfortable."

"We're just talking."

I made a pained face.

"What's wrong? Slick told me you believe all those stories. I'm surprised. I thought we were friends. I come in the store, and you take your time with me, like I'm the only customer you had all week." Jags shook his head and continued, sounding more serious. "Slick tells me you think I did something to Vinnie Pizza." He started laughing as if it were the funniest thing imaginable. His men laughed but kept their eyes on me as if waiting for me to make a move that needed their attention.

Thoughts of Jags beating his wife and his thugs putting a body in the Cadillac's trunk came to me in an alternating pattern. I began to shake.

"Don't say anything," Max said.

"I need to leave," I said in the smallest of voices.

"What's the hurry? I'll double what Waite pays you," Jags said.

"It's not the money. It's that I feel really uncomfortable here."

"Sitting here drinking coffee, you feel uncomfortable?" My words must have hit a sore spot for the corners of Jags's mouth turned down slightly.

"Tell him you need to get home," Max said.

"It's everything. The way your men responded when we got here. I couldn't live with myself if I learned later on that something happened to Vinnie Pizza."

"Can't live with yourself—pretty melodramatic. What do you think happened?" Jags said.

I scanned the room before speaking. I could not read Chops's expression behind his shades. Slick looked angry, and I imagined he would seek the first opportunity to inflict some pain on me. "This is not easy, Jags."

"Your voice, you sound like you're ready to start crying, like you're thinking of a eulogy for someone you love," Max said.

"I know what I know, and I can't look the other way."

"I like that in a man," Jags said and looked toward Chops, who nodded his approval. "Maybe we'd hit it off, you and me."

"I don't think so." My voice cracked.

Jags smiled a smug control freak smile. Slick unfolded his arms as if getting ready to act. Chops moved directly behind me; his being so near somehow sparked a degree of impulsivity that I had believed was drummed out of me during my first few years of school. "I saw a short, round man and a tall, thin man put a rolled-up carpet into the Cadillac with the PIZZA plate."

"And what, my friend Vinnie Pizza was in the carpet?"

I started three times before I could get out, "Yes."

Chops's stomach pushed on the back of my head, and Max made a horrified face.

"So you think I'm a murderer?"

I could not speak but gave a slight nod.

"Oh, that hurts, Rodney; it really hurts. Slick, get Vinnie the Pizza Man on the phone. Who do you think I am?"

"I don't know."

"For your information, the heavy guy you saw was the Pizza Man. He's got a heart condition, and that's why my man Joey Fangs gave him a hand putting the carpet in his car. The carpet was a gift. His wife loves the one we have in the den, so I got him one. Shit, Rodney, this hurts. I always liked you, but this hurts." Jags lowered his head for a moment and then shook it as if to chase away what he had heard and start over. "I was going to offer you a-once-in-a-lifetime opportunity. My accountant tells me I need to invest a good chunk of cash. I was hoping you would come to Italy with us, act like Ramona's personal travel guide. If all went well, I was going to offer you the chance to run a clothing store for me. I figure Haynesworth and Waite's is the best around here, and you seem like the best in that joint by a long shot. But if you think I'm killing people, you probably want nothing to do with me."

"It's Vinnie," Slick said, and handed Jags the phone.

"Hey, what's cooking, Vin. Got enough pepperoni? Listen, there was a misunderstanding when you left my place; I just want to make sure you're okay." Jags pulled the phone away from his face and said laughingly, "He says never better. You want to talk to him?"

"He's lying," Max said.

"No, that's okay."

"Vinnie, give your Lori a hug for me. Hope she likes the rug." Jags ended the call. "I think you owe me an apology."

"Apologize," Max insisted.

"You know, Jags, I don't believe that was the Pizza Man. I believe that heavy guy and Joey Fangs deposited the real Pizza Man's dead body into the trunk of the real Pizza Man's car and probably have fitted the body for a pair of cement shoes. I also believe what I read in the papers." My knees started rocking, but the more I spoke, the calmer I sounded.

Slick started toward me, but Jags raised a hand to stop him and started laughing. Whenever he began to stop laughing, he'd look at me and then begin roaring uncontrollably. After a minute or so, Slick also started laughing. "You got big fucking balls. You think I'm this badass Mafia boss, and here you are accusing me of killing someone and disrespecting me in my house, in front of my men. You really are something." Jags laughed so hard a tear came to his eye. He gave a slight nod to Slick, who pulled out his gun and pointed it at me. Then Jags made the biggest fist I had ever seen and swung at my nose. I turned, and the punch landed on the side of my head, knocking me out of my seat and onto the floor.

"Stay down—play dead," Max screamed.

CHAPTER 13

A WOMAN SCORNED

I lay on Jags's kitchen floor, held my breath, feigned death, and hoped. As I lay there, the full enormity of what I had done hit me. Just as Eleanor thought that she'd never in a million years be living in Hawaii, I could not have imagined the circumstances that would have put me in my present situation.

"Imagine this little fuck," Jags growled. He kicked me in the ribs, and I howled with more pain than I knew existed. "Listen, you little pip-squeak. Chops is going to take you for a ride in the country, some place only known to the birds and the bees; then he's going to strangle the life out of you. Now get up, show some class, and die like a man."

"Stay down," Max begged.

I was too scared to move. A bullet to the head would be far preferable to having Chops crush my windpipe.

"Slick, call Fat Freddy and tell him if he hasn't gotten rid of Vinnie Pizza to get back here because Vinnie's going to have company."

When he said "Vinnie Pizza," it all came to me. Vinnie Parello, Jags's codefendant, who reportedly ran a high-priced escort service and was a major player in the cocaine and heroin trade throughout New England. Everyone knew him as Vinnie Pizza because he operated out of his pizza parlor over on Grand Avenue, where a twenty-by-thirty foot sign on the rooftop of the two-story brick building read, "Vinnie's Pizza—one slice, and you're hooked for life."

An emotional Max spoke in a choked-up ghost voice: "I just want you to know I'm proud of the way you stood up to this crazy prick. Knowing he's about to have you blown out like a candle come bedtime, you stood up to him. Don't know where you get the balls. You had me thinking of great acts of courage, like John Wayne in *True Grit*."

I gave him a funny look.

"Believe me, kid; it's a compliment," Max said, and I could hear tears in his voice.

I heard Bruno hurrying toward us. He hollered, "Boss, Boss, your wife is here!"

Thinking of Mrs. Carmello as the cavalry, I scrambled to my knees and turned toward Slick, who was standing behind me with gun drawn. He began to speak on his cell phone.

"Freddy, the boss wants you to come back and pick up the gay salesman." There was a pause. "Yes, the guy they were taking to Italy. Yes, he's gay. Whatever, Boss wants a double dip at the quarry." A few seconds of silence followed, and then Slick asked Jags, "He wants to know if he they can take them to Primo Meats and turn them into sausage like our other friend."

"No, too messy," Jags barked.

"Boss, your wife is coming," Bruno said again.

"Nah, too messy," Slick repeated into the phone, and ended the call.

"Duct-tape this little shit, and take him out back. Put him in the shed with the lawn mower until Freddy gets here," Jags instructed. As Chops reached down to pull me up, Jags kicked me in the chest and knocked me backward onto the floor. Then he made a strangling motion with his hands to Chops. "I want him to remember that no one comes into my house and insults me. I want this little shit to remember my face as he buys the farm." He bent down, stuck his face in front of mine, and smiled.

"He's history," Chops said. He lifted me to my feet as if I were a suit filled with feathers, and snarled, "For a smart guy, you're a real dope." With me in tow, he started walking toward the back entry. Fear was in complete control. Every inch of me shook, and my senses were overwhelmed to the point where I welcomed death. I wanted to protest, but nothing came out.

"Rodney, we's going out back, and I'm going to tape you up and make sure you're safe. If you make trouble, I'll jam this down your throat," he said, sticking an enormous fist in my face.

"Scream, scream bloody murder! Scream like you were two and need your mommy," Max yelled.

I then heard Bruno say, "Boss, I couldn't stop her."

"Ramona," Jags said, sounding startled.

Ramona's voice halted Chops at the back entrance. We could hear what was unfolding in the kitchen but not be seen. Chops covered most of my face with his hand and pulled me close to him. I squirmed and offered some resistance, the equivalent of a worm about to be hooked. He put a choke hold on me. Any more pressure on my throat, and I would have been experiencing life the way Max did. Whatever strength I had was gone. Chops whispered, "One peep out of you, and you're dead, got it?"

I nodded.

"Ramona, put the gun away," Jags said in a quiet, confident way.

"You bastard, I gave you everything—I did everything you wanted. First, I lose our son, and now you treat me like this!" The voice was otherworldly, lost in anger. "I accepted everything. All the lost nights. I never questioned anything because you always treated me like I was the boss in this house. I was going to go to Junior. Misery likes company, and you certainly made him miserable, you son of a bitch. Then I said, 'Fuck you, Jags. I'm going to have my house, and you can take all your bums and go to hell.'"

"I'm sorry, baby." Jags sounded scared.

"Rodney, if he…" Max ran a hand across his throat and continued "you, I'll be looking for you on the other side. There's so much I want to tell you."

I nodded appreciatively. His presence made my impending death less frightening.

Chops gave me half a look and punched my already-bruised chin. I dropped as if my knees were gone. I felt as if my head had been dribbled down a flight of stairs. My front teeth were loose. I could taste blood. I wished I could see how bad I looked.

"Play dead," Max advised again.

This was quickly becoming easy for me. Chops scooped me up. In the rear entry hung a wooden coat rack with four large ornate hooks. Chops lifted me onto a hook and secured me to the wall, pegging my collar around the middle hook, which dug into my nape. Chops then opened a hall closet and came back with a roll of packing tape. He held my hands together with one hand and with the other wrapped the tape around my wrists several times. As he worked, I could hear Ramona screaming how Jags's hitting her was the last straw. Jags repeatedly told her he was sorry. I hung lifeless and acted as if I were unconscious, hoping Chops would leave and get caught up in the Ramona/Jags drama. Moments after he hung me, I could sense him leaving. I squinted, fearful that if Chops saw an open eye, he'd pound my hurting puss again. I saw him walk back into the kitchen. I immediately started trying to get the tape off my wrists. It seemed glued to my skin. Max looked as if he were straining, and after a few seconds, I whispered to him, "What are you doing?"

"Seeing if mental telepathy can get you down."

"Thanks," I said.

"Try to push yourself off," Max suggested, and began gyrating to demonstrate how I might be able to free myself.

"Put the gun down," I heard Jags say again.

"Tell them to put their guns down, Jags, or I'm going to shoot you right between your mangy, rotten eyes."

"Ramona, I'm sorry, dollface. I'm a jerk—forgive me."

"Tell Slick and Chops to drop their guns," Ramona demanded.

"Baby doll, all you need to do is put down the gun, and all is forgiven," Jags said, his confidence back.

"You'll let them kill me, won't you, you bastard!" Ramona said. I could hear a sad mix of betrayal and anger in her voice.

I pressed my butt against the wall and tried to push myself off. On the fifth or sixth attempt, I heard the sweet screech of a screw beginning to pop up from the wall. A moment later, I felt some sway in the rack.

"It's beginning to give, a little more, son," Max said, cheering me on.

With the screws loosening, there was enough play for me to use my feet, alternating right and left, to push off the wall. The rack made a great creaking noise, and I pushed with everything I had. The peg that held me snapped. Kerplunk. I fell forward; the rack dangled limply from the wall. The heavy thud of my flabby, one-hundred-sixty-pound body crashing to the floor served as a catalyst for the players in the kitchen, triggering a bang, bang, bang.

"Boss," Chops called.

"You did it," Max yelled excitedly.

"My shoulder—she fucking shot me," Jags moaned in disbelief.

"Get out of here, Rodney," Max said, trying in his best spiritual-being way to help me to my feet, which was like catching wind with a butterfly net.

I had already been in rough shape before my plummeting to the floor, and unfortunately my bound hands took the brunt of my free fall. I let out a nondescript groan and clumsily got to my feet. "I think my wrists are broken."

"She's dead, Boss. Two in the chest," Bruno said.

"How can this be happening?" Jags moaned.

"You need a doctor, Boss," Chops said.

"I loved her. Loved her bad, real bad," Jags said. "We had no choice. You killed my son's mother. Nobody knows what happened here."

"She tried to kill you," Slick said.

"Unbelievable…gave her everything. That's the thanks you get," Jags raged. "Shit, that hurts like a mother.

My shoulder, I didn't think she had it in her. A little lower, and bingo, I'm dead. This hurts like a mother. Can't be happening—we go from vacation planning to doing magic acts."

"Magic acts?" Chops asked.

"She's got to disappear," Jags said.

"You want us to put her with Vinnie Pizza?" Chops asked.

"Sure, but wrap her up in a blanket and tie a pillow-case over her face. I don't want anything to eat her eyes. If she'd missed me, and you didn't kill her, after a while, I'd have forgiven her," Jags said.

"That's love, Boss," Bruno said.

"Where's the gay boy?" Slick asked.

"In the hall," Chops said.

"When the fireworks started, I heard something out there," Bruno said.

Back on my feet, I turned to the closed back door. I cupped my injured mitts around the doorknob. Grinding my teeth from pain, I managed to turn the knob. As I opened the door, I heard Chops say, "He's hung on the wall, waiting to go bye-bye. If he fell off his perch, maybe he'll have a busted ass to go with his busted jaw." As I started out the door, I heard their laughter. Instinctively I started to run toward the drive-way. I thought that perhaps I'd get lucky, and one of the cars would be unlocked with the keys in the ignition.

What I didn't realize until my second stride was that running with one's hands taped in front of you takes a bit of practice. By the time I reached the driveway, I had figured out that by hunching forward as if trying to avoid extremely low-hanging branches, my balance wasn't half bad, and the visions of Chops's monster hands wrapped around my neck did wonders for my pace. Ramona's car was strategically parked, blocking the Lincoln that had brought me there.

CHAPTER 14

UP A TREE

"Here they come," Max shouted as I scanned Ramona's unlocked Mercedes for keys. No luck. Realizing that my best chance to escape death was gone, I thought, Keep your head down, and run for the street like there's no tomorrow.

"Come here!" Chops hollered from the edge of the driveway. There was a degree of authority in his command that caused me to hesitate for a second before taking off in a mad dash, screaming for help as I went.

"Shit, Rodney, he's got a gun," Max said, sounding as if it were only a matter of time before my spirit would be joining him.

I took one horrified look back. Chops looked ridiculous running with exaggerated bowlegs the way older, top-heavy men in need of new knees try to conquer distance quickly. His pace never rose above a labored trot, which from a safer vantage point, I'm sure would have seemed hilarious.

Bruno soon passed Chops, his form less tortured but still far from either accomplished or elegant. My only comfort was the thought that while Chops and Bruno were both champions of hand-to-hand combat, they were poorly designed for a prolonged footrace. It was a fleeting thought that succumbed to panic when I imagined them shooting me as I awkwardly galloped for the presumed safety of a stranger's home. "Shit," I yelled, running as quickly as my out-of-shape legs could handle. My head pounded, a miserable steady pain, reminding me of Chops's knockout punch. My throat felt as if I were a novice flame swallower who was destined to never master the act. Perspiration glued my shirt to my backside, and spots began to leak through my suit coat at the underarms. I ran, on the verge of tears, screaming over and over, "Help, killers, help, killers…"

When I hit the end of the driveway, I spotted an approaching motorist. I ran as quickly as I could toward the oncoming vehicle. Offering pathetic little waves from my shackled wrists, I widened my eyes in a plea of sympathy and yelled for help. The driver, a terrified middle-aged woman, swerved her little Corolla, just missing me. The car sped past me, causing the wind to whistle through me. I made out a groan from Bruno that sounded like a plea for me to stop.

"Crazy bastard," the woman hollered as she zoomed away.

In desperation, I called to her disappearing tail lights, "Please help me."

"They don't want to shoot you out here, cause too much attention," Max said.

"You see that?" I said, gulping in air and running toward the neighbor's house that sat diagonally across from Jags's property.

"Can't blame her—you look like a lunatic, a raving lunatic. Hands taped together; face swollen. Looks like someone used your head for a soccer ball. Your forehead looks infected. Those tattoos that little mutt gave you are starting to look bad," Max said. He then gave a look of despair. "Here comes the rest of the crew."

As I headed for the neighbor's front door, the black Caddy with Fat Freddy and Joey Fangs could be seen coming straight for us. I raced up the very wide brick steps of a home that seemed just a tad smaller than Jags's. I rang the doorbell, screaming, "Call the police." I turned to see a panting Bruno crossing the street, waving the Cadillac to a stop. Chops, wiping his brow, walked quickly a few feet behind him.

"Help," I yelled, pressing my finger against the doorbell. Westminster chimes played, but no one came to my assistance.

"Nobody's home, and the *Godfather* extras are getting closer," Max said.

I quickly surveyed the driveway and peered into a slender panel of engraved glass on the door. There were no signs of life. Down the stairs I bounced, running for the backyard and hoping no fences or walls separated the properties. My plan was to make it to the next street and find a brave Good Samaritan.

"No, no, no! Stay on the street where people can see you. Killers hate wide-open public spaces—stay on the street if you want to live," Max shouted as I ran toward the backyard.

I raced on, knowing one stumble, one bad break, and I was finished. Fear accelerated my speed across a perfect lawn that gently sloped downward. My throat and sides sent stabbing sensations that begged me to stop, but the idea of certain death pushed me forward. I ran through a ten-foot circle of marigolds and then a line of flowerless rose bushes; thorns snagged onto my pants. Nothing mattered but the killers, who thankfully seemed unable to gain on me. Behind the flower garden was a line of pampered Christmas trees from which bird feeders swayed in a random scatter that spoke of the possibility that normal people lived here. The thought gave me a fleeting sense of survival.

"Maggot, stop!" Those first words from Joey Fangs had the opposite effect, and I motored as fast as I could for the trees. My lungs were revolting, demanding an end to all this exertion. I looked back and saw Fangs about twenty yards behind me, followed by Bruno, who seemed to be losing ground. Chops placed a distant third. I disappeared into the tree line, branches at first easily parting with the force of my raised bound hands and then springing back and slapping the sides of my head as I passed. As if in league with Chops and company, the branches stung every bruise and cut of my battered face.

"Oh, shit, roses—son of a bitch," Joey Fangs yelled. I imagined Jags's goons tangled in the thorns and hoped they might be slowed enough to allow my escape or at least lengthen my lead.

I passed through the line of Christmas trees and into the backyard of another impressive estate. Taking center stage was a magnificent maple that held up the clouds. About thirty feet up, it split into three major arteries that supported a tree house the size of a one-car garage. A makeshift ladder of two by threes, snaked down the middle of the giant maple. My eye traced the ladder skyward as my legs pushed me upward. For some unknown reason, I viewed the tree house as a sanctuary.

"Where the hell are you going?" Max asked. Climbing, I kept my eyes focused on the tree house above, afraid that seeing any of Jags's men would send a shiver of fright that could cause me to lose my balance.

"There's somebody up there," Max said.

I began calling for help. With my wrists taped together, each step up the ladder put enormous pressure on my weak forearms and tired legs. After a few steps, my arms were unable to hold my torso steady, and I was forced to rest my belly against the ladder or risk falling backward. I imagined I looked like an enormous caterpillar crawling, without the slightest trace of grace, up this most unlikely of hideouts. A squirrel sitting on the edge of the house's roof spied down on me. I wished for some of his gravity-defying agility.

"You can do it; you can do it…" Max cheered me on.

"You're dead," Joey Fangs yelled from the tree line.

With five rungs of the ladder left, I noticed that the hole in the tree house floor looked like a tight squeeze.

"It's a dead end; you've painted yourself into a corner," Max moaned. "Worse thing you could've done. You've picked the perfect spot to be killed. What were you thinking!"

"Thanks."

"Just being honest."

"I need some optimism."

"You need a SWAT team."

"I'd take a cruiser with a pair of heroes," I grumbled.

"Make it easy on yourself," Joey Fangs called, his voice sounding close. With only three steps left to climb, I feared he would shoot me off the tree. The thought of crashing from such a height stopped me for a second.

"Got to move, kiddo; you're a sitting duck," Max said. Then, as if reconsidering our situation, he continued in a softer voice, "Don't be afraid; being dead isn't so bad."

With two rungs left, a scared teenage boy's face stared down at me. His skin was abnormally pale, reminding me of people who vigilantly guard against the sun. Thick honey-blond bangs fell in front of his forehead. He looked frail and stoned. Wires from an iPod plugged his ears. His eyes jumped about nervously. A friendly warm aroma filled the air. It reminded me of oregano. He took the buds out of his ears and screamed, "Get out of here!"

"Help, please, help me," I begged, my head about to pierce through the platform's opening. The boy stepped back and mumbled something. I gave what I hoped was a reassuring smile and pushed forward.

Whop! He kicked the top of my head. Fortunately, he missed a direct hit. I used all my strength, holding onto the rung for dear life, and miracle of miracles, I did not fall. "Call the cops, please," I shouted just as the boy took aim, lining up my chin like a football kicker preparing to start the game.

I pushed forward. My upper body floundered onto the tree house's floor. The boy retreated to the wall directly opposite me. "Look what you've made me do," he said, sounding angry and repulsed.

Below I heard Joey Fangs, "Shoot him in the ass."

"What did I make you do?" I said, crawling into the tree house.

"Somebody's up there with him," Bruno said.

"Shoot him, too!" Joey Fangs demanded.

The boy's voice cracked as he blurted out, "I'm a pacifist, and I just took a solemn vow to never, never, ever strike another person in anger, and here you come along scaring the crap out of me, and I kicked you. It's what I always feared. I must live alone, find a place, far away in the mountains." His voice trailed off and those last words, "far away in the mountains," seemed to be a condemnation.

"Right, and have the cops down here before we get him out of there?" Bruno said.

An excited Max chimed in, "Tell him to get ready to die because unless you figure out how to stop Murder Incorporated down there, his being a defective Quaker isn't going to amount to squat."

"You got a phone?" I hollered. His comment about pacifism only partially registered as I concentrated on the discussion taking place on the ground floor.

He nodded.

"Call the police," I said.

"You hear that?" Joey Fangs said. "'Call the police.' I had a bad vibe when Freddy told me about doing Vinnie Pizza. Now we got monkeys up a tree calling the cops. I should have listened to my gut."

"Can't," the boy said at the same time Joey Fangs was ranting.

"You have to, there are three killers down there, and very, very soon if you don't, you and me will both be dead."

"I've got over a pound of weed," the boy whispered. His eyes shifted to a shelf to my left that was nailed into the tree. I saw a blue plastic bin that measured maybe two feet by three feet. "It's my nest egg. I sell it, and next week I'm heading for New Mexico to commune with nature."

"Go up there and get them," Bruno said.

"You hear that? They're coming for us," I said to the boy.

"If they called the cops, I need to get out of here. The Pizza Man is in the trunk. You know what happens if they find him," Joey Fangs said.

"Where's Freddy?" Bruno asked.

"With Vinnie," Joey Fangs said.

"Then Vinnie is taken care of," Bruno said, sounding ticked.

"No, because he's thinking we're bringing this clown back to him. He can't think that the three of us is going to let this clown call the cops. So Freddy is sitting back there with Vinnie in the trunk, waiting like a sucker getting ready to be rung up," Joey Fangs said.

The boy and I edged close to the opening in the floor so we could better hear the conversation.

"Rodney up there?" an out-of-breath Chops panted.

"Yup," Joey Fangs said.

"Go get him," Chops gasped.

"He's got company, and they called the cops," Joey Fangs said.

"Gives us eight minutes, more or less," Chops said.

"I got to go tell Freddy to move the car. This is an amateur show, real amateurs," Joey Fangs said.

"Get your ass up there, and bring them down," Bruno demanded.

"This is your job. I only came with Freddy to do him a favor because he's been under the weather, and I owe him. He's paying me with a dinner. I don't climb trees and kill civilians for a measly dinner," Joey Fangs said.

The boy gulped. "Who are you?"

"Rodney Armstrong," I whispered. "Can you take the tape off?" The boy's face stiffened as if getting ready for a punch. "Please, it's us against them."

The boy sighed and motioned for me to show him my wrists. He began working the tape which had bonded into an impregnable seal with my skin. "Need scissors," he said.

"Where the hell are you going?" Chops asked.

"To tell Freddy to get lost with Vinnie Pizza," Joey Fangs said.

"Tell him to use some muscle," Max said.

"Get it started, and I'll use my teeth, but first call the police," I whispered.

"You can't leave in the middle; no one leaves in the middle," Chops said.

"Watch me," Joey Fangs snapped.

There was a pause, and then Bruno said to Chops, "You go get them."

"You should have made that skinny bastard get them," Chops said.

"He'll have some explaining, now get up there," Bruno said.

"You hear that?" I said firmly.

The boy pulled out his cell phone and hit 911. He then put the phone to my ear. After a voice on the other end identified himself as the police and explained that this call was being recorded, he asked for my name, where I was calling from, and the nature of the emergency.

"I'm Rodney Armstrong. I need help right away. Jags Carmello or maybe some of his henchman have killed Mrs. Carmello, and now they are trying to kill me and..." I looked over at the boy and whispered, "What's your name?" He violently pulled the phone away from me, ended the call, and gave a look of betrayal.

"What did you do that for?"

"I can't tell the police my name."

"There are killers down there who are going to be up here any minute." My voice rose as I continued, "And they're coming up here for one reason, to kill me because I know they've killed Jags Carmello's wife and one of their associates, a Vinnie Pizza. And then they will kill you because you witnessed them killing me. Do you get it?"

"Okay, okay, I panicked, sorry." He then began to pull hard on the tape and made some headway as one corner started to lift.

"What's your name?"

"Chance Lowenstein. My dad is the Lowenstein of Butler, Burns and Lowenstein."

"Me? What about you?" Chops said.

"Jags wanted you to do the salesman," Bruno said.

"He didn't say anything about climbing up a tree," Chops protested. "Look at that—its boards nailed to a tree. I don't think it'll hold me."

"Sure it will. Give it a yank," Bruno said.

"You can yank this," Chops said.

"We're wasting time," Bruno said.

"Then get your ass up there, because I don't trust that," Chops said.

"This is hard to say," Bruno started hesitantly, his voice quivering ever so slightly.

"What?"

"You tell anyone, and I'll kill you."

"What?"

"I'm afraid of heights."

"Don't pull that shit—like when we did the baker, and he jumped in the giant flour bin."

"I'm allergic; that's no shit. Thankfully, it's only to raw flour; that's how come I can still eat pasta and bread."

"It sounds like a crock, just like you being afraid of heights."

"If you don't go up there, I'm going to have to shoot him down, which will never work. Because unless they fall out of the tree, we still have to go up there and get them." There was a pause, and then Bruno said, "Do you want to go back and tell the boss how we had to let this kid go because I'm afraid of heights and you're still pissed at me after all these years for you having to dive into the flour bin to get that little asshole over on Jackson Street? Is that what you want?"

"Yeah, yeah, already, I'm doing it, but when this is over, we're having a sit-down with the boss. I'm getting too old for all the shit jobs."

"Just go, before the frigging cops come."

I jammed my taped wrists into my mouth and yanked as hard as I could. Chops had loosened several of my teeth, making my efforts useless and painful. "Can't do it." I gave Chance a look intended to draw sympathy. "The big guy down there belted me. My jaw is out of whack, and my front teeth can't bite like they should."

"Let me try," Chance said and began working on the tape. He rubbed his hands before starting as if drawing greater internal resources.

"Call the police back; you can make up a name," I said.

"This may all work for the best," he said, sounding far away.

"What are you thinking?"

"I'm still a little stoned, and after I get this off you, if there's time, we should roll up the biggest joint ever and just catch a buzz and forget everything. We think good thoughts. A constant outpouring of positive, life-affirming thoughts. When the killers get up here, we offer them a toke. Between the smoke and our karma, perhaps we win them over. You know, peaceful thoughts and a good smoke."

"Are you crazy?" I screamed.

"Hey, it's coming," In one easy motion, Chance liberated my wrists. I rubbed them for a few seconds and then opened and closed my hands, making fists.

"Knock this burned-out loony tune out on his ass," Max said, jumping up and down with excitement. Before he could say anything else, he fell sniffling to his knees with his head buried in his arms for protection.

"Never learn," I said, shaking my head.

"Learn what?" Chance asked.

"Drugs. You shouldn't be doing them."

"Phew, nice recovery," Max said, adding, "Sounds like they're losing patience with me. I didn't think that was so bad."

"Call the cops," I demanded again. Then it dawned on me that I had free use of my hands and my cell phone.

"My feet are too big to climb up this thing," Chops hollered.

"You got to put them sideways and pull yourself up," Bruno advised.

"It's made for kids," Chops said.

"That's not a kid up there. You just got to coordinate your arms and legs. Get into a flow. It's like dancing."

"Do I look like a dancer?"

"You know what I mean," Bruno snapped.

"If you're such an expert, why don't you show me?"

"I'll get seven or eight feet up, and the whole world will start spinning. If I don't come down when that happens, man oh man, you wouldn't believe it."

"What happens?"

"I don't know because I always come down."

"Bruno, I don't know if I can ever work with you again."

"Don't be a psychological bully," Bruno said.

"What the hell is that?"

"A person who uses another's emotional liabilities against them."

"You're watching too many of those talk shows."

"If you had a weakness, I wouldn't exploit it; that's the difference in us," Bruno said.

"Shit, man, that's what we do all the time."

"Not with each other."

There was a pause as Chops pulled himself up a step. Then he said, "That's why you liked Little Jags so much. Two of a kind, him wanting to save the world, always whining about something, and you of all people needing saving." His voice sounded raspy from the strain of climbing.

"You know how many people have phobias?"

"Giving this stupid shit a name doesn't make it less stupid."

"Do you?"

"No, and I don't care as long as the guy I'm counting on isn't one of them. Shit!"

"That's it—push with your forearms, and just move one leg up at a time," Bruno coached, sounding more like his old self. "Don't look down."

"Why not?"

"It makes me jittery."

"Definitely no more jobs with you. Jittery, for crying out loud. Jittery. That's it, you should be ashamed of yourself. From now on, Bruno, it's Jitts. Big Jitts."

"Jitts?"

"Jitts, that's what I'm calling you."

"I never said anything about that time in Vegas when you had the hots for that female impersonator. You said you liked them tall, remember? You were going to do her all night."

"I was drunk."

"Not the next morning."

"Okay, my lips are sealed, but we can't work together."

"That's it, Chops; you're halfway there."

I punched in 911. "I called a few minutes ago."

"Name?" a gruff officer on the other end asked.

"Rodney Armstrong."

"We dispatched an officer—should be there shortly."

"Great, but I have a more immediate need."

Max screamed, "Sweet Louise, get to the point!"

"Two or three of Jags Carmello's men are here trying to kill me and a young man who prefers not to be named." Chance gave me a shy thumbs-up. "We are in the backyard of—hold on." I turned to Chance and asked for the address.

Just as I was about to say "Twenty-Seven Wildberry Lane," Chops's enormous head emerged from the floor's opening. "Put that phone down!" he ordered in the nastiest voice I had ever heard. His interruption scared me the way only a near-death experience can. I dropped the phone. "Who wants to die first?" Chops let out a demented chuckle. Neither Chance nor I realized that Chops's monstrous shoulders could never fit through the floor's opening.

I was paralyzed with fear.

"Don't faint," Max barked.

Chance rushed for the cell phone but in his nervous haste, it slipped out of his hand, bounced twice, and slid along the linoleum floor. As if Chops were a cell phone magnet, it followed a direct course toward the floor's opening.

"Goodbye, cell phone," Max moaned as it disappeared down the hole. "Kick the gorilla's head back to hell."

I shook my head no and called to Chance, "Kick him in the head."

Chance shook his head no.

I waved my hands toward Chance and gave a worried look that I hoped he understood as meaning "what gives?"

"You do it," Chance said as Chops turned and twisted in an attempt to get more than his head and neck into the tree house.

"I can't," I said, stepping back as far away from Chops as possible. Chance gave me a strange look. "I've never hit anyone."

"Never?" Chance and Max both said.

"Never," I said, and tried to muster the inner strength to deliver as hard a kick as possible to Chops's huge head.

"There's always a first," Max said.

"Shit, Bruno, I'm stuck," Chops said.

"Kick him," Max urged.

"Can you shoot them?" Bruno asked.

"Nah, all I can do is spit at them. Get that skinny bastard Joey Fangs up here."

"This is a matter of life or death—hit him with something," Max shouted.

"You can do it, Chance. You kicked me without a problem."

"Yes, but you took me by surprise. Now I have my pacifist way in place. It would be a premeditated kick, I can't. I'm back to my true self."

"Tell him his true self will soon be a dead self," Max said.

"Chance, he's going to kill us." With those words, I charged toward Chops, cocked my right foot, and attempted to kick him square below the nose. Seeing my foot coming toward his face, the big man lost his balance and dropped fast and hard out of the tree.

"Chops! Shit, Chops!" Bruno yelled.

Chance and I hovered over the floor's opening. The sound of a distant police siren grew stronger. Chance and I exchanged thankful looks, like condemned men who just learned of their reprieve.

"Bruno, I can't move," Chops moaned.

"You hear that? The cops," Bruno said, bending over his fallen companion.

"Help me up," Chops urged. Bruno extended a hand, and Chops yanked hard on it. "Holy fucking shit, my legs—I can't move them." Bruno tried to lift Chops from beneath his underarms. "Get me out of here!"

"I can't. I told you once you started on those blood pressure pills to drop fifty pounds," Bruno said, grunting from the effort of trying to lift Chops.

"If I wanted a nag, I'd get married," Chops snapped.

The siren was noticeably closer.

"No sense in both of us getting busted," Bruno said, and stepped back from his partner.

"You can't leave me like this," Chops said.

"What can I do?" Bruno asked, backing away. "They'll be here any minute."

"You're right. Go ahead, go. Here, take my piece. Never thought it would end like this."

Bruno took Chops's gun and said, "Stay strong."

We watched from our perch as Bruno disappeared through the line of Christmas trees.

CHAPTER 15

MURDERS REAL AND IMAGINED

The siren grew louder and louder until we were certain the police would be pulling up to the driveway any second. As the siren's blare reached its most comforting saving pitch, Chance and I nodded little congratulatory nods to each other. But at that moment, the siren sounded just a tad less strident. Moments later the sense of our victory over dark, seemingly invincible forces drained away: the siren was weakening. I looked down at Chops, who was crawling along at a pace that would take him a week to make it to the line of Christmas trees. He was sitting up and using his arms to lift his behind and then propel his massive hulk forward. After each effort he groaned, sounding like a suffocating grizzly. The process moved him at best a few inches each time. But by the time he cycled through his system of movement, the siren was no more.

"Here! Come here—help!" Chance called to the officers he hoped were knocking at his front door or circling around the house. His calls alternated between a pained screech and a more pleasing hopeful soprano. I watched Chops's agonizingly slow progress. A forlorn Chance stopped calling for help. Chops collapsed in a heap maybe three feet from where the great maple began to stretch skyward.

"Where are they?" Chance asked.

"They're not coming," I said.

"They have to," Chance sounded as if he were about to cry.

"Get yourselves out of this tree," Max said.

"Call them again," I said.

Chance nodded and pulled out his phone, which made an annoying little beep. He looked at me with the saddest blue eyes. "Dead battery."

"Great," Max said.

"Your face is turning purply, and there's like all these little scrapes and welts and a small egg where your hair starts. Was that from my kick?" Chance asked.

"Lay a guilt trip on him," Max said.

"Maybe the egg, but the other stuff is from Chops and a loose-bowelled sausage dog."

"Was he nibbling on you?" Chance asked.

"No, it's a long story. We need to call the police and get out of here."

"You think it's safe?"

We both looked at Chops, who lay on his back. From the movement of his chest, I imagined he was trying to suck in as much wind as possible in preparation for another go at moving his great crippled mass.

"Is there a phone in your house?" I asked.

Chance squinted and wrinkled his nose, making a pained face as he shook his head no.

"Okay, but I don't think we have much to fear from him. Bruno took his gun."

"Careful, he might have another one on him," Max said.

Chance agreed with me and swung his legs down the entry hole. He gracefully descended the makeshift ladder, showing a sureness that gave me confidence that I too could descend this loft without receiving any further injury. As soon as I began my descent, though, fear gripped my heart and stopped my progress as I imagined joining Chops in a crumbled heap of broken bones.

Max said, "Today, partner, while you got a chance of getting out of here." As if he could read my mind, he said more softly, "You can do this."

I lowered myself gingerly. Each step down was done with trepidation as I clung to the rung above and searched with my right foot for the next step, reminding myself to turn my foot sideways before lowering myself.

"You can breathe while you're doing this," Max said teasingly. It was a comfort that the old Max was back, a sure sign that we were in less danger.

"Thanks. How much farther?" I asked.

"You're more than halfway." Then Max let out, "Oh shit!"

"Let me go," Chance screamed in terror.

I peeked below. Chops had the kid by an ankle and was pulling Chance toward him.

"I'm going to kill you, you little weasel. It's going to be slow and painful. I'm going to stuff your balls so far up your ass that they'll choke your heart," Chops shouted.

Shivers ran through me. I took two more steps down, guessing that I could leap without risking too much harm. I landed in an awkward sprawl, the force causing me to roll forward. My face kissed the sod. My nose, which somehow had managed to escape Caesar's claws, Chops's punches, and Chance's kick, was not so fortunate. Blood gushed out both nostrils. I instinctively raised myself up and threw my head back to slow the flow. I then pulled out my handkerchief and applied pressure to my nose.

Chops, unable to use his legs or lean his torso too far forward, was stuck in a weird position that reminded me of a Sumo wrestler attempting yoga. He wrapped his arms around Chance's legs in an attempt to bring the youth's upper body and head close to him.

"Head for the hills, Rodney," Max yelled, making a running motion.

"I'm going to rip out your throat, then your heart, and feed them to the pigeons. No, that's too easy. I'm going break your legs and then light you on fire," Chops threatened.

Chance dug his fingers into the sod. His legs wiggled about in the big man's hands; occasionally a foot would connect with Chops. The kicks elicited chuckles and comments comparing Chance to a little girl.

I got to my feet. My nose had stopped bleeding. I looked down at Chance struggling for his life. Chops had a crazed look.

"Get out of here," Max said.

Chops repositioned his hold on Chance, and I realized the professional killer was going to try to break the kid's ankle. I seized Chance by the shoulders and pulled with everything I had.

"You're next, you little fag," Chops snarled.

"Are you crazy? Get out of here!" Max yelled.

Chance looked as if he were losing strength. Chops grimaced, grit his teeth, and increased his pressure on Chance's ankle. I took a deep breath, screamed a guttural war cry, and yanked again on Chance's shoulders. Somehow he popped loose of the killer's grip. Chops was left holding one of Chance's shoes. The force sent me tumbling backward on my butt, with Chance's head driven into my belly. The back of my head hit the ground hard; my eyes watered, and my nose sprang a new leak, showering blood down on Chance, who let out a groan and started crying.

"You okay?" I gasped as we disengaged.

Chance wiped his face and stood up. "I thought for sure…"

Slowly, I rose to my feet, fearing I might pass out. I sniffled back some blood, hugged Chance, and then let out a wad of dark-crimson spit the size of a cantaloupe.

"Come back here, you little bastards," Chops said, his eyes bulging like a choking bullfrog. He then started waving Chance's sneaker over his head like a war club.

Chance and I took a few steps back.

"I'm gonna get up and kill you, you little bastards," Chops hollered in obvious pain. Like a big league pitcher, he let Chance's shoe fly. Whap—the sneaker hit my beat-up face. "Take that, you little fucker. Fight like men."

"Run, Rodney run," Max urged and pointed toward Chance's house.

I spied my cell phone behind Chops and circled around him. He followed me with his eyes and began taunting us. "Come on, you little queer boy. Come on, both of you. Come on, even without legs, I'll beat the two of you. Come on. I'll rip your arm off and beat the other little faggot to death with it."

I motioned to Chance to walk in the opposite direction in order to distract Chops. We quickly surrounded him. Chance, just out of the monster's reach, danced about in what the kid must have thought were menacing poses. I moved directly behind the wounded Chops, who readied himself for both a frontal and a rear attack by angling his body so that with a slight turn of his head he could see either one of us. He clenched his fists. I imagined him strangling me with one claw as he drove the other one through my skull. A goofy look came over Chance as he backed off and began picking up pebbles from around the roots of the great tree.

Chops turned his upper body toward me and spotted my cell phone. He began to make the most painful groans as he tried to pivot in order to get the phone before I did. I froze, afraid if I moved toward the phone, he would seize me, and that would be how this awful day would end, beaten to death by a crippled mob enforcer.

"What the hell!" Chops hollered.

I looked up and Chance was whipping pebbles at my worst nightmare. One, two, three, the nickel-sized rocks hit our enemy's face and neck. Chops turned his head and barked at Chance, who reacted by jumping back a good three feet. The pelleting created enough of a distraction for me to rush for the phone. I reached down to pick it up as Chops turned back toward me. He lunged for me, and his hammer paw hit my hand, knocking the phone out of my grasp once more.

"Shit!" I screamed.

"Punch him, Rodney," Max said, taking several swings at the air around Chops.

Chance jammed two fingers into his mouth and let out a bloodcurdling whistle that momentarily put the brakes on our adversary. I took advantage of his loss of focus and smoothly snatched the phone in an uncharacteristic instance of physical grace. The prize secured, I began jumping up and down, yelling in a high-pitched voice. "I got it, I got it."

"I'll give you five grand if you get me out of this mess," Chops begged and collapsed onto his back.

"Call the cops," Max said.

I nodded and punched in 911.

When the person on the other end answered, I was still frantic and trying to catch my breath. "The nature of the incident?" I said, "A man fell out of a tree. He's hurt very badly. I think he either broke his legs or screwed up his back." I gave the address and ended the call. I looked at Chance and said, "An ambulance is coming. I need to get out of here."

"I want to go with you," Chance said.

"No, you need to stay here and explain to the police how Chops and his friends chased someone into your yard and the stranger got away, but public enemy number one here fell out of the tree searching for whoever he was after."

"Where are you going?" Chance asked.

"Back to work, I guess."

"Call, see if your dildo boss is in any mood to see you," Max said.

"Yes," I said.

"Yes what?" Chance asked.

"Yes, back to work." I started to punch in the store's number, stopped, and called over to Chops, "An ambulance is coming for you, big guy. I hope you're okay, but even more, I hope I never see you again."

"Fuck you, you little weasel. When I get out of here, you're one dead little prick," Chops grumbled, losing the fierceness I had come to expect.

"I called an ambulance," I repeated, making sure he understood that I could have just left.

"Why do you care about him?" Max said.

"He's hurt real bad," I said.

Chance nodded, thinking I was talking to him.

"Who cares? He was going to kill you—still might," Max said.

"Chops, killing me, was it personal?" I asked.

"It is now, you little weasel," Chops said, shaking his fist and sticking out his middle finger.

"I hope your legs are okay and you change your ways in prison," I told him.

"If they give me thirty-years, when I get out, the first thing I'm going to do is find you and make you suffer until you're begging me to kill you," Chops said.

"Kill him while you got a chance," Max said.

I shook my head and finished making the call to work. "Lana."

"Rodney, where are you?"

"It's a long story."

"Well, there are detectives here looking for you."

"Detectives?"

"Detective Milano and Parker. I told them about that crazy man. They're here investigating your murder.

I thought when you went to lunch that that nut found you, and this time he didn't miss."

"Murder?"

"Yes, they're investigating your murder."

"Murder? How?"

"The maniac who tried to kill you went after somebody else. A Dinky Horton, who escaped and called the police. When they arrested this nutcase, Spike Drake, he admitted to shooting you. Said he put a bullet between your eyes."

"That's great."

"Great!"

"Yes, that they arrested Spike."

"Where are you?"

"I'm on the other side of town."

"Are you in trouble?"

"I don't know."

"This is not good, Rodney."

"But as long as no one else tries to kill me, I think everything will be fine."

"Who else would try to kill you?"

"It's just one of those days."

"The detectives are coming over here. Do you want to talk to them?"

"No, tell them I called, and I'm on my way there." I ended the call and nodded to Chance. "I got to get out of here and back to work."

"Man, where did you come from? We just escaped certain death from the nastiest man on earth, and you want to go to work?"

"The kid's right," Max said.

"There are detectives there investigating my death."

"I saw that on TV once. A dude predicted his death, and no one believed him. Let's go back up the tree, roll the biggest joint ever, and smoke our brains out." Chance gave a contented smile and pointed with his eyes to the tree house.

"It's nothing like that," I said.

"Maybe it is like that. Maybe you're going to die, and I'm supposed to guide you through it. Maybe I get a chance to do something for you," Max said, somewhat excitedly.

I frowned at Max and asked Chance, "Do you have a car?"

"Nope, but I got a Vespa."

CHAPTER 16

RODNEY ROCKS

"Remember, as soon as I get out..." an immobile Chops moaned as Chance led the way to the garage.

"Wait here, I'll open the garage," Chance said, as calmly as a Wal-Mart greeter on a slow day.

"Hurry up," I said as he went inside.

"Are you all right?" Max asked.

"I think I'm numb."

"Never in a million years does a guy like you beat those guys."

"It's not over yet."

"They know you called the cops, I'm sure they're scurrying for cover."

I shrugged, and the garage door opened. Everything about the garage was as I had imagined it would be. It was immaculate. Tools that looked like they were never used hung neatly along the back wall. Between a sparkling clean sit-down lawn mower and an equally glistening snow blower was a Vespa, a shade of yellow that would stand out in a bushel of lemons.

I wondered how safe it was. Chance smiled, strapped on a helmet with a peace sign decal on one side and a marijuana leaf on the other, and climbed aboard the toy like scooter. Wearing an expression I took for pride, he eased the Vespa away from the lawn equipment. "Special paint," he said, and nodded.

I nodded back and for a moment thought, yes, this is how I'll meet my end.

"There's a helmet over there. It was my girlfriend Andi's. But we're history; the relationship is as broken as that busted-up killer in my backyard."

"Oh." I wanted to say more but felt the urgency of our circumstances weighing on me. The thought of Chops regaining the use of his legs and surprising us stifled the desire to ask if the scooter was safe for the two of us to travel across town.

"She is thinking big-time conventional nonsense now." Chance threw up his arms in a what's-the-use way. "Where do you need to go?"

Andi's helmet was a swirl of pinks and lavenders accented with tiny shimmering stars. "Haynesworth and Waite's, on Main Street."

"Just what your image needs," Max said, sneering at the helmet.

"Place makes me nervous. My dad gets his suits there. Can't imagine anyone being there every day."

Somehow the idea that I may have waited on Chance's father made me feel even more uncomfortable, as if my getting his son involved in near-death experiences were a violation of some unwritten trust between customer and sales associate. I again spied the helmet and gave a little grunt, more of dismay than protest. I could hear the ambulance's siren. Chance started the scooter. It made a sweet humming sound, which was the first bit of evidence that trusting this reefer-mellow young man might be okay. I looked at Chance for encouragement. He smiled and asked, "You like the color?"

I thought, they'll see us coming, and nodded.

"Special paint. Andi picked it out—cost extra." Then he shouted, "Come on, baby, let's get her rolling!"

"Do I really need this?" I asked, looking skeptically at Andi's headgear.

Chance shrugged and said, "The way your head has been getting bonged? It doesn't seem like it's your lucky day."

"The kid has a point," Max said.

"Is there enough room?" I asked, squeezing my aching head into the helmet.

"Just get on as close as you can. You are the first guy to ride with me."

The remark brought Dinky to mind, and I hesitated.

"Once he gets going, just hold on and keep your eyes closed," Max said.

"Come on this will be awesome. Riding away from killers, like in movies when the heroes leave a world of danger after winning the day."

"Right," I said, wondering when this nightmare would end.

Chance tapped the side of his scooter and yelled, "You ready to fly?"

"What the hell?" I grimaced, joining Chance on the small seat. He rolled us forward. As we cleared the garage entrance, he hit the remote opener, and down came the door. Max sat beside me on nothing but fresh air as if an invisible extension of the seat existed. Of the three of us, he was by far the most comfortable. The helmet pressed down on my skull, punishing my aching head. With the first real acceleration, I fell back and then over compensated and pushed forward. My nose jammed into the nape of Chance's neck, and my chest banged into his back, remaining there as if we were one.

"Easy, partner. You feel like Andi, only heavier."

I lifted my head and told myself to keep my face off him.

"Hang on to the back bar or my waist," Chance giggled.

Between his advice and the repulsion I felt from the forced intimacy, I raised my arms up and away from him, which caused me to lose my balance. My torso dipped first to the left and then to the right, scaring the crap out of me before I clutched onto Chance's middle.

"With that helmet, you better hold onto the bar, because you look like an ad for some low-budget, kinky boy-man love movie," Max said.

I turned back to see Max laughing as if he were having the time of his life. I carefully removed one hand and found the bar and clasped it firmly.

"No problem hanging onto me. I'm used to Andi back there. She'd snuggle a little tighter, so don't get all freaky if you want to hold onto me. I don't mind."

"He should mind," Max said.

"I thought I was going to die back there," Chance said, and shuddered.

I nodded, thinking, He only knows a drop from the sea of insanity that's been my day. For some reason, I suddenly felt very fortunate.

When we reached the end of the street, an ambulance with lights flashing whipped around the corner. Chance gave the EMTs a thumbs-up and turned toward Jags's street. As we passed the Carmellos' mansion, I tried to keep my eyes straight ahead, but Max pulled my attention toward the scene of the crime with, "Man oh man, there's three cruisers." I glanced over and felt a surge of confidence, thinking that with Jags bleeding and a dead Ramona somewhere to be found, I was the least of the crime boss's problems.

In seconds, Jags and company were safely behind us. Chance cruised at about thirty miles an hour down quiet residential streets. The wind slapped against us, and I felt with each passing intersection that I would safely get back to my life.

"What was that with Chops?" Max asked.

"What do you mean?" I whispered, thinking my words would be lost to Chance as long as I kept the volume down.

"You sounded like you were really concerned about that bastard's health."

I motioned with my head toward Chance.

"Don't worry about him, between the putt-putt's purr, the wind, and the helmet, there's a better chance some stray mutt will see me and freak out than mush mind hearing you. So what gives with you and our equal opportunity killer back there?"

"I couldn't just leave him."

"Why the hell not?"

"Because he was helpless and hurting. Who knows what would have happened to him?"

"Is there mud between your ears or something? This is the guy who nearly breaks your jaw, and if he had his way, you would be dead, probably getting dumped in a deep lake or buried in woods so thick nobody but the worms would ever find you. And the entire time you were with him, he had you scared shitless, and you're worried about him being helpless? Rodney, as long as a guy like that is breathing, believe me, he's a far cry from being helpless. You should have dropped a boulder on his head."

"This may sound weird, Max…"

"Believe me, the longer I'm dead, the more I realize everything is at least a little weird."

"If I just left Chops back there, never mind killed him or added to his misery, I would never have forgiven myself. I'd be sick."

"*You're nuts!*" Suddenly Max raised his arms to defend himself and buried his head into my shoulder. "Okay, okay, I get it. He's right."

"Wow," I said as Max lowered his arms.

"Wow?"

"You said, 'He's right.'"

"It was my mother again. She said you were a beautiful person, and I needed to be like you. She's been telling me that caring for others, no matter how bad they are, is the way we're supposed to be. That I pissed away my life trying to con people and find the next party. That my selfishness will cause me to lose my life."

"Wow, she said that?"

"And more. Since we landed in the tree house, she's been lecturing me in between your close calls with Chops. My being here was caused by her pleading to get me to see how miserable my way of life has been. She said my way would cost me everything." Max shrugged and raised his shoulders as if surrendering. His voice trembled, and I thought he was going to cry as he continued. "I am so sorry for all the terrible things I've done. I wish I could have another shot at it because now I know. Forgive me, please."

Then—poof—Max was gone, and I heard him say, "Thank you, son. Now I understand. Thank you."

A warm, reassuring feeling came over me. It lasted probably only seconds, but it felt, satisfyingly, much longer.

We were now in the midst of a large, cozy middle-class neighborhood; most homes were about a quarter of the size of Jags's. My phone began vibrating, and that comforting secure feeling vanished. Hanging onto Chance with one hand, I gingerly pulled my cell phone from my suit coat's inner pocket and spied the number. Home. Between helmet, wind, and Vespa's hum, I knew attempting a conversation with Elizabeth would be fruitless. I tapped Chance on the shoulder. For some reason he thought I was simply congratulating him; he raised his left arm, clenched his fist, and made repeated pumping motions. I tapped him again, and he nodded but kept moving forward. I again tapped him, this time with both my hand and head. He slowed the scooter. "Pull over," I hollered. After some momentary confusion on his part and my yelling at him several more times, he finally did.

Once we were parked by the side of the road, I said, "Home called." Chance looked bewildered, and I continued, "Have to take this; it could be important."

"Do you think those guys who wanted to kill you will come after me?"

"It'll be a long, long time before they make it out of prison," I assured him, frantically hitting the receive button on my phone.

"You trust the prisons and courts?" Chance said skeptically.

I nodded, waving the phone at him.

"You trust them holding Jags Carmello?" Chance asked, running a finger across his neck. He shook his head before saying, "My father said Carmello has pull at City Hall, the courts, the governor. My father says, 'Nothing ever sticks.'"

I turned away from the kid, not needing anymore doubts about the odds of surviving my new relationship with Jags and answered the phone.

"Mr. Rodney, you must come!" Elizabeth excitedly screamed.

"Is it Mother?"

"It is everything!"

"Elizabeth, calm down."

"This woman is saying things, things that if true, I don't know what will happen to you."

"Is she still there?"

"Yes, I'm in the bathroom, and your mother is sleeping in front of the television, exhausted with worry."

"What's the problem?"

"Your mother is certain that you and Beatrice are lovers. At first that made her heart smile. But the longer Beatrice talked, your mother's face went from something I had never seen in her, joy, to her usual 'the storms are coming our way', to finally pain, great pain."

"What gave her the idea we're lovers?"

"Beatrice. She has not stopped talking about you. How you saved her from some Spike character, risking death for her, a common whore."

"She said that?"

"Yes, and she said you promised to help her get to Baltimore. That you are going to pay for her trip."

"Yes."

"She began talking about how you met. That you were talking to yourself about work problems. Your mother told her that was nonsense because you are the top salesman there. Beatrice said all she knows is what she knows, and you told her you were mad at your boss. Then your mother, she turned to me and said, 'Like last night, he was on the floor babbling to himself. My Rodney has cracked up,' she said and then looks at Beatrice and says to me, 'Maybe this is how he'll get rid of me.'"

"No, it's nothing like that," I interrupted.

"Your mother asked her if you were going with her to Baltimore. Beatrice looked surprised and laughed for a long time and then said that would be rich, you two slumming down there. She laughed until tears came to her and she said, 'What the hell, if he's game.'"

"Don't you worry, I'll be home in a while and explain everything. Let me talk to Beatrice."

"Please be careful, Mr. Rodney."

"It's a little late for that."

"What has happened?"

"Nothing, don't worry."

I could hear Elizabeth leaving the bathroom and soon after handing Beatrice the phone. Beatrice came on and excitedly said, "Your mother is a trip, man. She thinks you and me are running off to Baltimore and that you're bonkers."

"She gets an idea and forget it. But I have some news," I said. I was trying to sound cheery, but I was so worn out, I probably sounded ominous.

"News?" She sounded alarmed.

"Yes. The police arrested Spike. They have him for trying to kill Dinky, and he confessed to killing me."

"What a nut job."

"Yes, detectives want to talk to me; they're waiting for me at work."

"Don't mention me!" Beatrice screeched.

"Holy moly, you blew my ear off."

"Sorry, but you can't mention me," Beatrice repeated, taking it down a notch.

"Why?"

"Because the police will arrest me just to have some fun, and I get stir crazy in like five minutes inside a cell."

"Well, what can I say?"

"You can say anything you want as long as sweet Bea here is not any part of what you tell them."

"I'm not a good liar."

"Shit, man, practice!"

"Afraid I'll blow it."

"Okay, okay, tell them you don't know why he came after you. They got him admitting he tried to kill you. What more do they need?"

"No idea. Never been part of a murder investigation, real or attempted."

"He tried to kill you, Rodney. That's the only thing you need to tell the cops." There was a pause, and then she asked, "You still going to help me?"

"Yes. Let me talk to Elizabeth."

"You're the bomb," Beatrice said, and I could hear her laughingly give the phone to Elizabeth. I told her I might be a little late.

"Mr. Rodney, I need you," Elizabeth whined.

"It's been a busy day, and I might have some things to take care of at work that could cause me to be late."

"Mr. Rodney," Elizabeth whined.

"I'll get there as soon as I can."

"We will wait until eight; then the chicken will start to burn even if I lower the heat, or it will get cold if I shut it off and let it sit. It is so good right out of the oven. We can't wait any longer than eight. And I do want you to enjoy this feast; you sound like you could use a good meal. I will do my best to keep it ready for you, seven would be ideal."

I ended the conversation by thanking Elizabeth and telling her not to worry. I put away my cell phone and then looked around.

"Chance, Haynesworth's is just a few blocks away. I can walk from here."

"Man, I don't mind."

"Police are waiting for me, and you don't need to get mixed up with that."

"Right. What should I say if the cops are waiting at my house?"

"Just tell them a stranger came running up your tree house, trying to escape from some guys who wanted to kill him. And you helped him escape by giving him a ride downtown."

"Do I know your name?"

"No."

"Do I know anything else?"

"The less you say, the better off you'll be."

"Man, you rock!" Chance wrapped his arms around me and hugged me for a while.

CHAPTER 17

CLOSING TIME

I approached Haynesworth and Waite's with the late-afternoon sun fading fast. Glimmers of light danced on the glass panel of the store's door, and I caught sight of the mess I was.

"Yipes!" I stopped and took inventory. Caesar's tiny claws had left a string of reddish welts across my forehead as if my head had been stuck in an angry hornets' nest; thanks to Chops, the left side of my face was swollen purple; my hair needed a comb, my eyeglasses sat askew on my nose, with a noticeable downward left slant; the right sleeve of my jacket was torn at the shoulder and elbow; and my trousers looked as if I had spent the afternoon planting flowers in muddy soil. I thought, Would you buy a suit from this man? Would you even ask him for the time of day?

I ran a hand through my hair and played with my glasses for a second, returning them to my nose marginally less crooked. As I opened the door, I became overwhelmed, realizing that somehow I had managed to escape death three times, and the sun hadn't set yet.

"Rodney!" Lana hollered and came running to me from behind the checkout counter.

I put a hand out to stop her, which she ignored and charged forward. She wrapped her arms around me and whimpered, "Dear God, what happened? I've been worried sick." Her embrace felt marvelous. I imagined the way an underdog who becomes champion must feel when the match is finally over, and he is in the arms of that one special person in his life.

Before I could answer, Van, who was a few feet behind Lana, said, "You look like someone used your head for a hammer."

"Are you all right?" Lana asked and released me.

"Yes, I never felt more alive."

Van sneered, "You look like hell."

"Well, Van, it's like this, I've faced certain death more than once today. The men who wanted to blow out my brains or choke the life out of me are either locked up or in the process of getting busted, while all I have are minor injuries which, in a few days, will be worn like medals, earned combating street thugs and mobsters."

You would think I had said "never felt better" as Van began, "You owe me big time." I wore my confusion like a photo ID badge. He continued, "After being an hour late from lunch, I had to report you to Mr. Waite. After that nasty Buffington fiasco, his first reaction was to fire you as soon as you showed up. I went to bat for you. Reminded him of your loyal, dedicated service, of how you always put work first. I told him of your way with customers, assured him that you'd have a good reason for everything. Saved your butt, Mister."

"Everything?" I asked.

"Besides Buffington, there's the prostitute. We like to think Haynesworth and Waite is a piece of paradise in a sea of despair. But having the likes of that one in here— well, somehow I managed to save you." Van cleared his throat in an overdone "excuse me" fashion.

"Thanks," I said, truly appreciative until it dawned on me that if I were canned, Van and Simon would be forced to handle every customer until a new person was hired and trained. Mr. Waite was very particular about whom he brought into the business. Van had suffered for about a month after I was hired before Mr. Waite felt comfortable with me taking the lead when a customer walked into the store. I don't think Van had it in him to bounce from customer to customer, sometimes for hours at a time with not so much as a chance to blow your nose.

"Then Detectives Milano and Parker showed up," Van said, and a new level of gloom crossed his face.

"And?"

"The publicity, a pimp involved in a shoot-out with a Haynesworth and Waite man." He pursed his lips and continued, "No, no, no, that simply won't do. Don't know what will happen, but my money is on you showing up at the unemployment office in the very near future."

"Shoot-out implies I was shooting back."

"Technicality," Van said, nodding triumphantly.

"He's the victim. He could've been killed!" Lana exclaimed and wrapped an arm around my elbow. "What happened to your face?"

Before I could answer, Van said, "Thankfully he didn't get killed, because that's the kind of news that would put a real dent in holiday sales." He smirked. I resisted the urge to choke him.

"Really, Van?" Lana said and stamped her foot.

"I mean, even the prostitute coming here. She's involved with the shooter, and why do two seriously questionable characters find their way here? And of course, as predictable as milk going bad on its expiration date, your friends unleash deadly chaos. Hmm," Van said, looking down his nose.

"So am I fired?"

"Of course not," Lana blurted.

"The detectives asked all kinds of questions about the shooting. They're upset you didn't call the police like any innocent man would."

"He was in shock," Lana said and stepped between Van and me.

"So am I fired?"

"The detectives have been planted in Mr. Waite's office for over an hour, waiting for you, I imagine. All I can say is it doesn't look good for you, Mister," Van said.

"What are they doing with Mr. Waite?" I asked, knowing that getting fired wasn't the worst thing that can happen to a person.

"Don't you listen? They're waiting for you. They are investigating the shooting." Van's smirk grew into an even more disagreeable smile.

"Will you stop grinning?" Lana barked at Van, who seemed taken aback by her assertiveness. "There's nothing funny here," she said in a much softer tone, as if realizing she had seriously overstepped her bounds.

"Tell me, Van, is there any sense in me going in there and talking to those detectives?"

"Rodney! Civic duty," Lana scolded me. "But what happened to your face and clothes?"

"It's more than you should know. But, Lana, I was kidnapped, beaten, and forced to hide in a tree."

Lana shrank with every word I spoke.

"Believe me, I did nothing wrong,"

"I do believe you."

"I hope you'll still join us for dinner tonight."

"Rodney, you're safe now, and I can't think of anything I'd rather do than have dinner with you. Now go talk to those detectives. I'll be waiting for you."

"Thanks," I said, giving a mischievous smile as I knocked on Mr. Waite's door. Waite told me to enter, and I detected a phony lightness in his "Come in." Golf balls and putter had been put away. He stood behind his desk. Two rather large men in tight-fitting, poor-quality suit jackets sat in the wingbacked chairs in front of the desk. They turned toward me. The one nearest was a fifty-something light-skinned black man whose head seemed too big for his neck. He looked at me, and I sensed he was upset about waiting so long for me. I would learn that he was Parker. The other detective, Milano, was a bit younger with a shaved head. I took him as the kind of man who must have excelled in hockey or football not too many years ago.

"Rodney, these are Detectives Parker and Milano," Mr. Waite said as I entered. "What happened to you?" he asked as he sat down.

"Long story," I said.

Mr. Waite motioned for me to take a seat in the chair directly in front of him and between the two detectives.

"We have time," Parker said.

His voice reminded me of Elizabeth for there was a hint of what I took for a Jamaican accent. "Are you from the islands?"

"What islands?" Parker asked.

"The Caribbean."

"No, I'm one hundred percent American," Parker snapped as if I had offended him. Milano smiled and wrinkled his nose momentarily as if fighting off a sneeze. "That's funny to you?" Parker fired at his partner.

"You, you're funny. Never seen a guy so sensitive about things," Milano said, crossing his arms as if to signify he was tired of battling with his partner.

"You sound like my mother's caretaker, Elizabeth," I said, mustering my best placating voice.

"So now I sound like a woman." Parker glared at me.

"No, it's just a hint of an accent. I think it sounds terrific—gives you an international persona." I tried to show I meant no harm, but my face, my jaw especially, hurt so badly that my attempt at a smile was more of a grimace.

"What's that face for?" Parker shouted.

"I was smiling."

"That's no smile," Milano chimed in, sitting back in his seat as if enjoying the scene unfolding before him.

"That's the face of a man who likes getting smacked," Parker said.

I brought a hand to the side of my face for emphasis and said, "I got beaten up, and my head feels like someone is walking on it. I guess my smile muscles are kaput."

"Who beat you? Spike Drake?" Milano asked, getting down to business.

"No, they call him Chops."

"Chops?" Parker, Milano, and Mr. Waite said at the same time.

"Yes. Don't know his last name. He works for Jags Carmello."

"Jags!" Parker and Milano said, almost leaping out of their seats. Then Parker said, "You got mixed up with Angelo 'Chops' D'Otto?"

"We weren't formally introduced," I said.

"Tell me about you and Chops," Parker demanded.

"It's a long story." I said again, looking at my watch.

"You in a hurry?" Milano asked.

"Yes, it's my mother's caretaker, Elizabeth. She'll worry." I cast a glance at Parker and attempting to smooth over any hard feelings, said, "The one you sound like. It's funny, isn't it, the way people keep traces of their native accents? You know, how people years after emigrating still have a hint of their native tongue? I like it."

"Maybe that beating screwed up your ears. I have no accent. I was born here. Now get on with your Chops story," Parker said, leaning toward me. I felt his enormous head crowding me.

"Sorry," I sighed and tilted away from him. "But I do have to be home by seven. Elizabeth is making her special midnight chicken."

"Maybe we should find out about Spike Drake." Milano changed the subject hesitantly. He then took out a notebook and began writing.

Wanting to protect Beatrice, I decided to keep the focus on my meeting Chops. "I was minding my business when Chops and Jags's bodyguard Bruno..."

"Bruno Liberti?" Parker interrupted.

"We've always been on just a first name basis," I said. Parker looked at me as if experiencing indigestion. I paused, and he nodded for me to continue. "They insisted I go with them to Jags's home."

"That's where you've been?" Mr. Waite said, shaking his head disapprovingly.

"Didn't Jags call and explain things?"

"No, but that's your responsibility, not a customer's," Mr. Waite said.

I so much wanted to give him the bird.

"So you went to Jags Carmello's place against your will," Milano asked.

"No force was used, but if you know Chops and Bruno, they are very convincing fellows." The detectives nodded. "When we pulled up to Jags's home, problems were afoot."

"'Afoot'?" Parker said.

"That means 'about,'" Milano said.

"I know what it means. I just don't associate Chops, Bruno, and Jags with problems afoot. They're more the-shit's-hitting-the-fan kind of guys," Parker said and shrugged.

"Yes," I continued, "Vinny Pizza was being put into the trunk of his car by Fat Freddy and Joey Fangs."

"Vinny Pizza is dead?" Milano said.

I nodded. I felt pretty good regarding my position as eyewitness to what I imagined was enough to put Jags and the gang away for a long time.

"How do you know it was Vinny Pizza?" Parker asked.

"His license plate. And later when the shit did hit the fan, getting rid of his body was discussed in detail."

"So you saw things and heard things about Jags killing the Pizza Man, and you're here talking to us?" Parker asked.

"Yes. After Jags talked with me about going to Italy with him and his wife."

"Going to Italy?" Milano repeated, shaking his head as if he hadn't heard right.

"Mrs. Carmello had her heart set on the trip for years. She figured Jags wouldn't be very good company for her, you know, taking in the typical touristy sights, so she wanted me to be her traveling companion. They think I'm gay and would be safe with Mrs. Carmello." I lowered my voice and leaned toward Parker and said, "But I'm not gay."

"Is that relevant?" Parker asked.

"To me it is very relevant."

"Get on with your story," Parker said, in a way that made me feel like I was a bunion being squeezed into a tight pair of wingtips.

"Anyway, I couldn't leave my mother; she's in failing health."

"Sorry," Milano said.

"She's been hanging on for so long; it's hard to imagine anything else."

"You were saying about vacationing with Jags and the wife," Parker interrupted.

"Yes, no way could I go sightseeing with Jags, Ramona, and Bruno. Even before seeing them deposit Vinny Pizza into the trunk, I knew I wanted nothing to do with Jags, so I refused the free trip. But he was very intense about my going. You see, he had a big fight with his wife over their vacation. Jags not used to being told no, and he hoped if I went to Italy with them, it would smooth things over with his wife. Instead, I kind of lost it with him over the whole Vinny Pizza deal. I underestimated how scary he can be."

"You lost it with Jags, and you're here telling us about it?" Parker sat back, and a smile crossed his face. "Are you on drugs?"

"Only prescription ones."

"Go on." He then looked over at his partner and asked, "You getting all of this?"

Milano nodded.

"I insulted Jags and accused him of killing Vinny Pizza. Jags ordered Chops to take me out and strangle me. He wanted me to die slowly remembering how I insulted him in his home. They were supposed to get rid of my body along with Vinny's. Fat Freddy and Joey Fangs had already left with Vinny. As this was happening, Ramona Carmello returned home in a rage, wanting to kill Jags. Chops knocked me out, duct-taped my wrists, and hung me on a coat rack. His interest in Jags and Ramona's little war saved my life."

"How so?" Milano asked, looking up from his notebook.

"Ramona, and this is what I pieced together from my perch on the coat rack in the back entry way, shot and wounded Jags. Slick, Jags's driver, or Bruno shot and killed Ramona. As soon as the shots started, I managed to pull myself free from the coat rack. Jags called for Fat Freddy and Joey Fangs to come back and pick up Ramona and me. I took off running, and fortunately Bruno and Chops are not aerobic-exercise enthusiasts. I escaped running across a couple of streets and through some yards, finding refuge in a tree house."

"Of course," Parker said.

"That was another stroke of incredible good luck. Turns out that Bruno is afraid of heights, and Joey Fangs, who physically seemed the best candidate to climb up the tree and kill me, was only doing Fat Freddy a favor and wasn't really getting paid for his services, so the task of climbing up the tree and killing me fell to Chops, who really needs to lose a good hundred pounds. Thankfully, Chops's great heft was too much, and he lost his grip, falling like Humpty-Dumpty. He may have a broken back. Once my wrists were freed, I called the police, which got Bruno running. When I realized it was safe, I came down from the tree house and made it here as soon as I could, knowing I was seriously late from lunch."

"Wow," Parker said.

"Earlier today, in what appears to be an unrelated event, did a one Spike Drake attempt to kill you by firing a handgun at you?" Milano asked.

"Hold on a minute," Parker hollered, and raised his palm, halting Milano. "I'm going to call downtown."

Milano nodded.

"Give me Captain Boswell; this is Parker." As Parker barked into the phone, Milano began reviewing his notes. Mr. Waite gave me a quizzical look in which I thought I detected a sense of awe at my story.

"Captain, I'm sitting with a Mr. Rodney Armstrong. He tells me that he witnessed Jags Carmello's wife getting killed in a shoot-out at Jags's place. He also tells me that Chops D'Otto and Bruno Liberti kidnapped him and tried to kill him. No, that's not all; Mr. Armstrong also heard a conversation involving the death of Vinny Pizza." Parker sat back in his chair and listened. Every minute or so he would say, "I see." When his conversation with Captain Boswell ended, Parker turned to me and said, "You, Mister, are one lucky bastard."

"It doesn't always feel that way," I said.

"Let's wrap this up and go downtown," Parker said to Milano. "Because there are some bigger tunas to fry." He let out a little laugh and smiled at me, and for the first time in his presence, I didn't feel like my fly was open. "You'll be reading the papers tomorrow: 'Jags Carmello arrested in connection with the deaths of his wife, Ramona Carmello, and an associate, "Vinny Pizza." Also arrested in connection with these deaths are Angelo "Chops" D'Otto, Bruno Liberti, Freddy Cantucci, and Joey "Fangs" Lofanti.' Because right now four of them are under arrest. Jags and Chops are at the hospital under guard, and there's an APB out on Slick, who was last seen driving toward Connecticut."

"Wow," Milano said, and asked again, "Did a Spike Drake also try to kill you?"

"I'm not sure of his name but a muscular, thirty-something white man did try to blow my brains out." Keeping Beatrice out of this was all I could think about.

"Why did he want to blow your brains out?" Parker asked, sounding supportive now. I wished he had called down to Captain Boswell when I first mentioned Jags.

"A misunderstanding, but I'm okay, so if you have other things to hold him on, I really don't want to get involved."

"Somebody tries to kill you, and you don't want to get involved?" Milano asked.

"I'm sure I've nothing to fear from this Spike fellow."

"What makes you so sure?" Parker asked.

"Like I said, it was a misunderstanding."

"About what?" Parker asked.

"He thought I was becoming romantically involved with his girlfriend." I hoped this was reasonable and did not jeopardize Beatrice.

"He's a pimp," Parker deadpanned.

"Really?" I said, trying to sound surprised without overdoing it.

"And if you were involved with one of his girls, we'll let it all slide if he in fact tried to kill you. In fact, if you testify against Jags and company, I'm sure we can arrange for you to have one hell of a party," Parker said, and winked.

"No, like I said, he must have got me mixed up with someone else."

"It would be a great help if you came down to the station and identified the man we are holding and give us a written statement," Milano said as he chewed on his lower lip for a second.

I then turned to Mr. Waite and asked, "Am I fired?"

"Fired?" Milano said, giving Mr. Waite a look of disbelief.

"No, no, no. Given what you've been through, I can understand your tardiness," Waite said. Looking first at Parker, and then Milano, and lastly at me, he said with a tone of confidentiality, "I strongly advise you, Rodney, to cooperate with the police."

"If what you are saying about Jags and the gang is true," Milano said.

"Oh, it's true," I said.

"And if you're willing to testify in court, the city— no, the state—will be forever in your debt," Milano said.

"A real hero," Parker added in a way that felt like sarcasm.

"Imagine, a hero working here," Milano said, staring across at Mr. Waite.

"It gives one pause," Mr. Waite said.

"I'm sure it will be good for business," Parker said, not hiding his distaste for Mr. Waite.

"Okay, but I need to be home by seven...."

Parker interrupted. "No promises, but how often do you get a chance to put away a pair of maggots from opposite ends of the local crime world? Carmello goes bye-bye, and Chops, Bruno, Fat Freddy, and Joey Fangs join him. Shit, man, this is probably the most important thing you'll ever do."

"Yes, of course, but..." I said.

Before I could voice my mounting fears over what I might be getting into, Detective Parker sprang from his seat and thrust a large knuckled hand at me. I meekly accepted. He squeezed hard and yanked me to my feet. "Rodney, you put that bastard Carmello away, and this city owes you, owes you big time."

I swallowed my reservations regarding Jags's revenge, for at that very moment I could feel Max proudly looking down on me, and I thought, Act like a man. "Before we go down to the station, I need to make a couple of calls."

"Calls?" Parker said, releasing my hand from his bear-trap grip.

"Home," I said, and then turning to Mr. Waite, I added, "and Mrs. Buffington."

"Good idea," Mr. Waite said.

"Make it quick, and not a word about what you saw or heard—not a word about what you're about to do," Parker said. His face turned deadly, like a mother wolf protecting her pups.

Parker kept his eyes on me as I took out my cell phone and called home. The more he stared, the more I felt the need to alert Beatrice about Spike's recent developments. As his gaze grew in intensity, I became increasingly anxious. I found myself gradually turning away from the detective. Elizabeth answered on the second ring. I glanced at Parker, and sure enough, his eyes were fixed on me. He smiled as if, I believe, to communicate his newfound admiration for the man who would put Jags Carmello away, but his hard-boiled persona made him look uncomfortable.

"Thank God it is you, Mr. Rodney." Elizabeth's voice allowed me to breathe more easily. "Your friend Beatrice is in the kitchen playing solitaire. I am working around her, making the tastiest dish you have ever eaten." Elizabeth whispered, "She keeps asking me if I want to play gin. I have no time for such nonsense."

"It's fun." I could hear Beatrice in the background.

"So," I said.

Elizabeth burst out, "I do not have time for games. She makes me mad and nervous. And your mother is worried about last night and happy again thinking you are this one's boyfriend. I think during her nap she must have had a sweet dream about that one. Tell me again there's nothing between you."

"You are crazy," I heard Beatrice yell.

"No, no, it's nothing like that."

"Good, because you are a very nice man, a good man. You can do much better."

"Thank you, Elizabeth. How is Mother?" I again looked at Parker, who tapped on his wristwatch but then smiled as if to tell me it was okay for me to keep talking.

"She's sleeping in front of the television. You must get here." Elizabeth lowered her voice so much I could barely make it out. "I do not trust this woman. She makes me nervous. You must talk to your mother about last night."

"I don't steal from friends," Beatrice hollered.

"Elizabeth, I've been under a lot of stress, and last night I was a little drunk. Then when I saw someone who looked like an older version of me, it got me wondering about my father. But I saw my doctor today, and I feel much better. No more drinking for me." It seemed so much better than saying my father's ghost had been my companion for nearly twenty-four hours. I looked at Parker, who seemed disappointed. I mouthed to him, "Not true, will explain."

"Some men can't handle their liquor, and their liquor ends up handling them in ways that makes me want to cry. This one you must never drink with."

"I can't imagine that ever happening."

"Good, for she is the kind of woman who will destroy you."

"What has she done?"

Parker cleared his throat. I ignored him but felt my stomach tighten.

"I told her until you come home, she is to stay in my sight. I told her if anything is stolen, it is my job that is on the line. She said she's…"

"I may be a whore, but I don't steal from friends," Beatrice screamed. I could hear anger and imagined Mother's presence was the only thing keeping fists from flying over there.

"She's right there?" I asked, surprised by Elizabeth's rudeness.

"Rodney, make it fast," Parker said.

I waved him off without looking.

"Yes, I told her she needs to be where I can see her at all times."

"Let me talk to her."

I could hear the phone being exchanged. It did not sound like a graceful handoff.

"Your girl here is a hell of a trip," Beatrice said.

"You okay?"

"I've been insulted by crueler crows and bigger bitches than this Jamaican jackass."

"You are a disgrace, a total disgrace, and I don't trust you," Elizabeth boomed in the distance.

"Tell me something I don't know," Beatrice said, and began clucking like a chicken.

"She means well."

"Bullshit. She's an uptight Aunt Jemima. Don't look at me that way. If this was somewhere else, I'd dance on your head and piss in your face."

"This is the kind of person you welcome into your home!" Elizabeth barked, and then added, "I should wrap you up into a ball and bounce you out into the street where you belong."

"Rodney," Parker snapped. "Let's go!"

"Listen, I won't be home until later this evening. Not sure if you and Elizabeth will survive until then. You don't have to worry." I stopped, not wanting to raise Parker and Milano's suspicions.

"What you talking about?"

"Your problem is over."

Beatrice paused. "You can't talk?"

"Right, but he's gone."

"Who's he?"

"Your biggest worry."

"Spike's going away?"

"Right, I'll be late, have to take care of some business."

"Spike get himself arrested?"

"Right. If you want, I could meet you tomorrow and give you what you need."

"For Baltimore."

"Yes."

"Tomorrow?"

"Yes, you tell me where."

"He's really arrested?"

"Yes."

"The bus station at noon."

"Sounds good. Let me talk to Elizabeth. I'll tell her you're going."

"You're the best," Beatrice said, and gave Elizabeth the phone.

"Wrap it up," Parker said, and poked my shoulder.

"Just a second."

"Mr. Rodney."

"Elizabeth, she's leaving, and I may be very late, so if you can save me some of your midnight chicken for when I get home."

"I will try to keep it warm and moist. Thank God that one is leaving."

"This call will be much shorter, I promise," I said to Parker as I ended things with Elizabeth. He shook his head and moaned like a wounded walrus.

"You got women troubles?" Milano asked.

"Don't get me started," I said, and looked toward the ceiling as if calling to heaven for assistance. I then briskly asked Mr. Waite to get Mrs. Buffington on the phone.

"You got problems with the sauce?" Parker asked.

"No, it's just better for my sick mother to think that than think I was hallucinating."

Parker's eyes grew to the size of walnuts, and I wished I had come up with something less dramatic. "She thought I was, but I wasn't. Believe me, I don't."

"Hallucinate?" Mr. Waite asked.

"Yes, I don't."

"But your mother thought you were?" Milano asked.

"I thought I saw my father who I never met, and that got my mother thinking I was seeing things." Man oh man, why did I say anything about drinking?

Parker looked skeptically at me.

"I was a little anxious last night, but I took some Prozac, and it did the trick."

"You sure you can handle going up against Jags and the boys in court?" Parker asked.

"After today, piece of cake."

Parker looked at Mr. Waite, who motioned he was using the phone. "Don't take all day," Parker said, and sat on the edge of Mr. Waite's desk.

"Hello, Bev; Duncan Waite here. How are you doing?"

"Better, but a long way from good, Dunk. Our little Caesar is home, thank goodness, but severely traumatized. This was quite the ordeal for him."

"Just calling to find out if there was any news. Glad to hear he's home."

"That's so kind of you."

"Rodney wants to talk to you. He feels just awful. Here he is." Mr. Waite hurried the phone to me.

"Mrs. Buffington."

"Oh, Rodney, what an adventure Caesar took. Trouble is, since I retrieved him from the most adorable young lady you'd ever meet, he's been hiding under the bed in one of the guest rooms. When I approach him, he whimpers, and then when I attempt to comfort him, he growls. It's most disconcerting."

"But he's home and not hurt?"

"No physical injuries that I could see, but the psychic harm, I believe, is considerable."

"Give him a day. I'm sure he'll bounce back."

"No, no, no. I called Dr. Daisy Denmark. You may have heard of her. She's written several books on dog trauma. Her latest is *If Dogs Could Talk: Bringing Out the Inner Canine.* She's an international authority in the area of dog psychotherapy."

"Dog psychotherapy?"

"That's what I call it. Dr. Denmark refers to it simply as pet therapy. But after speaking to her this afternoon, she reminded me of my personal therapist."

"Pet therapy." I was trying to process this while Parker made hurry-up gestures.

"Yes, she believes Caesar may have experienced some type of trauma earlier in his life, and somehow seeing you this morning triggered a relapse. Animal PTSD, she called it."

"Really."

"I have an appointment tomorrow at ten sharp. She's squeezing me in between a depressed Boston terrier and a boxer who lost his bark following a weekend of being forgotten in his owner's car. Sounds criminal, forgetting seems unlikely, but who am I to judge? Dr. Denmark believes it may be good if she sees Caesar as soon as possible. She wants to eventually have Caesar relive, as close as possible, yesterday's trauma."

"Glad to hear he's back with you."

"Rodney, it would, from what Dr. Denmark said, be an enormous help in Caesar's treatment if she could see how Caesar reacts to you. And it would mean the world to me."

"Oh." I was regretting the call.

"Yes, Dr. Denmark asked if it were possible for her to observe you and Caesar interacting, and I didn't know what to say. But now you, out of genuine concern for my precious little darling, called to see how we're doing. How fortuitous!" There was a prolonged silence. I dreaded what I knew would come next. With the urgency that parents use when pleading for their children's lives, she said, "Could you accompany us to his appointment? I'm sure it will accelerate the healing process."

"Accompany you?" I barely managed to repeat her request.

"Whatever she wants," Mr. Waite said, and crossed his legs confidently.

"Yes, I'll pay you for your time. Pick you up wherever. It would mean the world."

"I don't believe this," Parker said as he stuck his watch in my face.

"Hold on, please." I put the phone against my chest and looking at Mr. Waite, said, "She wants me to go with her and Caesar to a pet therapy session."

"Pet therapy," Milano repeated.

"Sounds like a case of affluenza," Parker said, walking away, as if disgusted.

"Pet therapy," Mr. Waite said.

"A Dr. Denmark believes Caesar may have dog PTSD."

"What a load," Parker hollered from the opposite end of the office.

"When?" Mr. Waite asked.

"Tomorrow morning." Mr. Waite nodded. "I think I'll need to take tomorrow off."

Mr. Waite hesitated, and Parker jumped in from across the room, "This kid has been through hell. If he puts Jags Carmello away, the city should give him a parade."

"He must be exhausted," Milano said.

"Yes, Rodney, of course—take tomorrow off. Make Mrs. Buffington happy."

I raised the phone to my ear and made arrangements to meet Mrs. Buffington and Caesar at Dr. Denmark's office. Mrs. Buffington thanked me repeatedly and told me how Caesar meant the world to her.

"Can we please go now and take care of Jags and Spike?" Parker asked.

I nodded, and Mr. Waite led the way out of his office with me sandwiched between Parker and Milano. It was now closing time, and Lana, Van, and Simon were standing about the checkout counter near the front entrance. For some reason Lana thought I was being arrested. As we neared, she sprinted toward us, stopping directly in front of me. "What's happening here?" Her voice cracked, and her eyes were full of sympathy.

"I need to go to the police station," I said. I could feel my head swimming with emotion.

"Why?" Lana shouted and put a hand on my forearm.

"It's okay," I said.

"You're not in trouble?"

"No, Rodney here is a hero, a real honest-to-good-ness hero," Mr. Waite crowed, wearing a proud smile as if he had directly contributed to my escaping death and defeating Jags.

"Phew!" Lana let out.

"I'm sure you'll read about it in the papers," Milano said.

"What about tonight?" Lana asked me.

"This could be a while," I said.

"Can I go with you?" Lana's eyes darted between me and the two detectives. I gave her an encouraging smile and looked at Parker for an answer. "For moral support," she beamed, and wrapped an arm around my waist.

"Sure, why not?" Parker shrugged.

My cell phone rang. It was home. "I should take this," I said.

"Of course, locking up a maniac pimp and destroying the city's main crime family can wait," Parker said, starting off in a growl but ending in a much softer tone.

"Isn't he something?" Lana said, staring at me.

Parker, Milano, and Waite all nodded.

"Hello."

"Rodney." It was Mother. "That long-legged black girl left. Her and Elizabeth had words. It got pretty ugly."

"It's okay. I'll see her tomorrow."

"Elizabeth says she's a prostitute."

"I know."

"You getting mixed up with whores, bringing them home?"

"It's a long story, but she's just someone who needed help."

"And who are we, the Red Cross?"

"It's just something I needed to do."

"And last night, I'm still not sure all your screws are tight enough for you to think straight."

"You were right; I was drinking. Dr. Hitchfield warned me that my medications for anxiety could cause a reaction if I drink too much."

"Why should I believe you?"

"Because I'm your son, and despite everything, I love you, and you love me."

"You drinking now?"

"No."

"You need to take better care of yourself. Don't worry so much."

"Yes. Thank you."

"Elizabeth's cooking up a storm. She's making a mess of my kitchen."

"It sounds great. Tell her to save some for me and Lana; we'll be late, but I wouldn't miss her midnight chicken for the world."

"Lana?"

"Yes, she works with me."

"Is this different then the thing you got going with Beatrice?"

"I hope so."

"Me too."

The End

ABOUT THE AUTHOR

Carlo Morrissey is a retired school psychologist. He was motivated to write his latest work of humorous literary fiction, *If You See Your Father, Shoot Him,* by the belief that good people can rise to the occasion to become unlikely heroes. He teaches sociology and psychology at Quinsigamond Community College in his hometown of Worcester, Massachusetts.